AF399356

Sylvia Gresina

Mission in Rome

novum pro

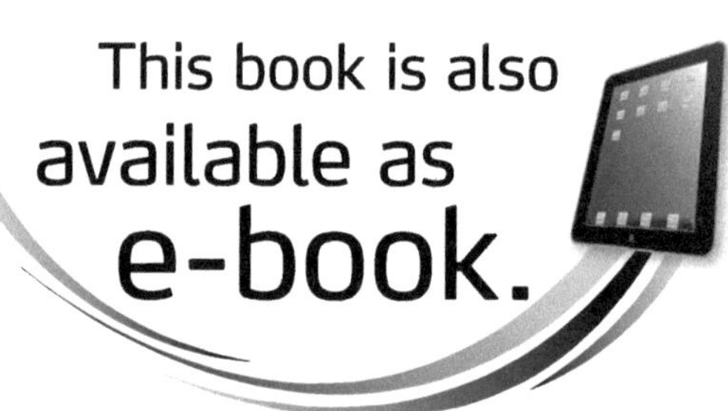

www.novumpublishing.com

© 2024 novum publishing

ISBN 978-3-99146-657-4
Translation: Agnes Balassa
Cover photos: Diana Eller,
Michael Piepgras,
Anton Aleksenko I Dreamstime.com
Cover design, layout & typesetting:
novum publishing

www.novumpublishing.com

CHAPTER ONE

The Arrival

It was a splendid day, full of sunshine, when KLM flight 829 landed in Rome. While the weather was typical for Rome, Lorain found it positively miraculous, having just departed a wet, foggy morning in the Netherlands. After picking up her luggage, she spotted the Institute's driver, who was waiting with a placard in hand bearing her name. After a brief friendly greeting, he helped her with her heavy suitcases and led her to the parked car. During the drive he extolled the joys of working with his colleagues at the Institute in the Eternal City, while she admired the magic of Rome, enchanting monuments appearing one after another. Lorain had been to Rome several times before on scholarships. But this time, having completed her PhD as an Art Historian, the prospect of a five-year mission in Rome with its potential adventures filled her soul with excitement.

Crossing the city from via Magliana to Villa Borghese, they turned onto via Omero in Valle Giulia heading toward Lorrain's new home, the Holland Institute. Lorain knew it well. The Institute (Istituto Olandese di Roma) conducted research in history, art history and archeology and was charged with promoting Dutch culture in Italy, expanding relationships among Dutch and Italian Universities, and organizing conferences, exhibitions and concerts. During her previous visits, she had never, even in her wildest dreams, hoped that one day she would be working for the Institute.

The Institute's Receptionist, Umberto Bianchetti, promptly announced Lory's arrival to the Director, Paul Veltmann. Paul was a tall, well-built, handsome man in his sixties. His gray hair was barely noticeable due to his fair complexion. He received his new Artistic Secretary, sitting at his desk with pipe in hand, reminding Lorain of the captains of medieval Dutch ships.

"Welcome Professor Hennes," the Director began. "I hope you had a good trip. Since you've been here several times before, I'm hoping Antonio's driving didn't alarm you too much. Have you ever driven in Rome?"

"Not yet," Lorain responded directly but courteously. "During my previous visits I went everywhere on foot or by bus or other public means."

"Don't worry! You'll soon get used to the rhythm of Roman traffic. I've planned for us to meet tomorrow morning to start your new job. In the meanwhile, let's get you settled into your flat." Veltmann pushed a button on his phone and called for the caretaker.

"I'd like to introduce you to Gianluigi Colombari, our Caretaker. Gigi can hand any technical or mechanical problem you might have during your mission here. He will show you to your flat. And please remember that my wife and I are looking forward to you joining us for dinner this evening, in the residence on the other side of the garden opposite the Institute. You can't miss it."

With that, they exchanged good-byes.

Lorain was ready to retreat to her apartment after the excitement of the day. Her flat was appointed with Louis XVI furnishings and had a view of the quiet Villa Borghese park, from where the whispering sweet sound of a fountain could be heard. The living room, at the end of the spacious hall, was bathed in sunshine with a kitchen at the far end. The southeastern corner opened to two bedrooms, each with its own bathroom. From one side of the living room, she could see the Viale delle Belle Arti, with its never ending traffic, providing a constant reminder of the pumping rhythm of the city. Lorain had just enough time to shower and put her cloths into the wardrobe before heading to the residence to meet the Veltmanns for dinner.

Paul and his wife, Ingrid, greeted Lorrain warmly. The dinner was excellent and they enjoyed the evening, discovering mutual interests, experiences, and even friends in common. Lorrain's only mild concern was that Ingrid seemed to have taken a maternal interest in her, making her wonder if Ingrid, who was not otherwise employed, might try to take care of her.

The next morning, Veltmann met Lorain in his office at ten sharp to introduce her to her new colleagues and review her job responsibilities. Beyond the Driver, Caretaker, and Receptionist, whom Lorain had already met, there was the Secretary, Julienne Becker, the Scientific Secretary, Nickolas de Backer, and the Accountant, Daniel Prick. Then, Veltmann showed Lorain to her office and presented her with the annual cultural calendar, which she was to manage.

"You know, Professor Hennes," Veltmann began, "your job is critical to the life and reputation of our Institute. So, I expect your complete attention and focus on every detail. I will expect you to share the details of every event you are responsible for planning, in advance, for my approval."

"Yes, Sir," Lorain responded. "I will do everything possible to support the Institute's cultural mission."

"Perfect. This's exactly what I wanted to hear. Now, I'll let you get started."

Not all aspects of the job were new to Lorain, although her previous scientific and research oriented jobs had not provided her much opportunity to organize and execute cultural events. She eagerly began reviewing the cultural calendar to plan her approach.

At noon Gigi, offered to show her the nearest supermarkets and confirmed that she could use the official Institute car for shopping until she bought her own. In case of necessity, with the Veltmann's permission, she could also avail herself of the institute's Driver, Antonio, and Veltman's Mercedes.

After filling her pantry, Lorain started work on an upcoming contemporary music concert, writing introductions for the musicians. Before arriving in Rome, she had contacted the Institute's Secretary, Julienne, to send out invitations, due to the timing of the concert.

Lorain was also expected to open an exhibition of modern Dutch painters organized by the Director and her predecessor. She set off to the Institute's gallery to oversee the installation of the paintings and ensure everything was in order. Entering the gallery, she noticed Nickolas de Bakker standing in front of van Gogh's self-portrait, admiring it. She went and stood beside him.

"Stunning, isn't it?"

"Ah, it's you!" he responded. "Yes, it really is extraordinary. I just got lost in its beauty."

"I'm glad that the Institute's Scientific Secretary also has an interest in art," Lorain responded. "I have to admit that I also like scientific conferences, historical presentations, and evenings of literature, even if these aren't part of my professional portfolio."

"That's good for our common work. I was told you also have a degree in archeology. I got my degrees in history and philosophy. I think it's important to appreciate other disciplines, especially in the work we do. Afterall, you don't have to be a musicologist to organize a good concert, as long as you consult with the right experts. Well, I shouldn't keep you from your work. I'm sure you've got a lot to do with this exhibit opening the day after tomorrow. But, I wonder if we might continue or conversation over lunch sometime in the near future, if you're interested?"

"How very nice of you! Sure, why not? Although, right now I'm consumed with my current tasks and getting up to speed in my new job, so my week is pretty full. But I've planned to go sightseeing this weekend. I hardly wait! Ancient ruins bear such a special attraction for an archeologist. Maybe, if you'd like, you could join me then?"

"That's an excellent idea! I'll look forward to it and we can have lunch together while we visit the sights. Which day were you planning?"

"Let's meet Saturday morning at nine o'clock at the garden's gate."

"All right, I'll see you there. And good luck with the exhibit!" He added and left Lorain alone with the paintings.

The concert and the exhibit were both great successes. The exhibit displayed a collection from the Museum of Fine Arts in Amsterdam, providing an exclusive opportunity to showcase masterpieces of Vincent van Gogh, Jan Toorop, Jan Thorn-Prikker, Kees van Dongen, Jan Sluyters, Jozef Israels, Johan Barthold Jongkind, Jakob Matthus, the Willem Maris brothers, Antoine Mauve and Hendrik Mesdag, among others.

Saturday morning, when Lorain arrived in the garden, Nickolas was there waiting for her. After a quick greeting, they set off to Rome's historical center. According to Lorain's plan, they began their tour with the Roman Forum, then climbed Traianus' Column to enjoy the view of the ancient ruins around them. Then, they continued their tour to the Colosseum and crossed the marvelous Palatinus Hill, finishing with the House of Livia to enjoy the rare example of sophisticated ancient wall paintings. They reached the Pantheon just after two o'clock in the afternoon. The Pantheon was Lorain's absolute favorite ancient structure, if an archeologist can pick a favorite from among so many incredible monuments. Finally, they arrived at the Hotel Minerva's rooftop terrace, settling in at a table with a panoramic view, and ordered a well-deserved lunch.

After Lorian made her selection, Nickolas commented, "I see you like 'frutti de mare'. I love seafood, too."

"Yes, I'm a great fan."

"Since we'll we're getting to know each other and will working at the Institute together for the next five years, would you mind calling me Nick?"

"All right, Nick," Lorain smiled. "You can call me, Lory! But at the Institute it might be better to use our formal names to keep things professional."

"Sure. As you wish, Lory. And congratulations on the success of your first two programs. You deserve all the acknowledgements the organization received for them."

"Thank you! That's very nice of you. I put a lot of effort into my work and try to do the best I possibly can."

After an enjoyable lunch, they returned to the Institute. Having enjoyed the day, they agreed on their next date, the following weekend to visit the Via Appia Antica by bicycle, Roman style.

The next week in spite of her heavy schedule, Lory managed to escape to walk in the Villa Borghese, near the Institute, and to visit every archeologist's dream, the Villa Giulia Etruscan Museum. The walks helped Lory clear her head and focus more deeply on her work, a skill she would need to remember all of the new people, places and information necessary for her new job. Luckily, she was particularly well organized at work and in her private life as well. She relied heavily on a diary in which she recorded upcoming tasks and important information about the past events, rather than her thoughts and emotions.

The Villa Borghese, next door to the Holland Institute, provided an excellent spot for an afternoon break. The Museum and Gallery Borghese is located in a Casino built in the 17th century in Baroque style. Although it's not very large, it houses one of the most beautiful and remarkably valuable artistic collections in the world, established by Scipio Borghese. His bust, carved by Bernini, can be found there. The collection features many famous statues, including *Paolina Borghese* by Canova, *David, Apollo and Daphne*, as well as the *Abduction of Prosesrpina* made by Bernini. All these treasures are surrounded by ancient roman mosaics and statues. The artistic atmosphere of the Gallery can be summed up by listing some of its most moving paintings, like the *Crucifixion* of Pinturicchio, *the Woman with Unicorn* of Raffaello and the *Last Judgement* and the *Ascension of Christ* of Fra Angelico and masterpieces of other painters like Caravaggio, Correggio and Tiziano.

Lory adored this Park for its artistic value, and also for its rejuvenating natural environment. Sitting beside the fountain or the lake, she enjoyed reading and found it easy to put her thoughts in order and work out plans for upcoming cultural programs. She wasn't surprised when, on one of her peaceful afternoon relaxations in the park, Nick appeared and said hello to her. He admitted that he also liked to visit the park for many of the same reasons she did. Lory invited him to sit down beside her and they discussed the beauties and hidden characteristics of the park. After a while they were just sitting side by side in silence admiring the swans swimming on the lake and the children running around it. Lory hadn't felt like this in a long, long time, sitting contentedly with someone without saying a word.

The week passed faster than she had expected. Her typical week progressed at an exhausting pace, organizing two concerts and a lecture, on average. Lory was looking forward to her weekend visit with Nick. Saturday morning, she set off in a hurry to their planned meeting point at the Via Appia Antica where Nick was waiting for her with two rented bicycles.

"Hi!" Nick greeted her. "I thought you would never arrive! If we weren't keeping our friendship secret from our colleagues at the Institute, we could have left together."

"Hi," Lory responded. "You're probably right. But you know how people can jump to conclusions."

"As far as I'm concerned, they can believe what they want. If we enjoy each other's company, it's nobody's business what type of relationship we have."

"You're right," Lory responded, looking away, embarrassed. To change the subject, she suggested, "Let's start our excursion and enjoy what may be the most authentic archeological site in Rome. I'm looking forward to exploring the everyday life of the ancient Romans. That's why we're here, right?"

So, they got to their cycles and began to ride along the world famous road together discovering ancient monuments and soaking in the sunshine.

After admiring the soundness of the ancient road, they visited the two most famous catacombs: San Sebastian and San Callisto. It was well after two o'clock when they reached a lovely restaurant, perfectly suited for the historical environment. They relaxed a bit and reviewed the menu looking forward to their meal.

"It's been a beautiful day," Nick said sitting relaxed in his chair.

"Yes, for me, too," Lory answered, briefly concentrating on the wide range and variety of delicious menu options offered by the restaurant.

"We really should do this again. There are plenty of sights to see, in Rome, so let's insert an excursion like this in our weekly plans. What do you think?"

"All right, why not! I need to use the lady's room. Would you please order me a spaghetti alle vongole veraci and for the second course calamari with green salad," Lory asked as she disappeared.

When she returned, her meal had just arrived, enticing for her with an irresistibly inviting smell. Nick's food had also been delivered, but, being polite, he waited for Lory to start eating. In typical Roman style, alla Romana, the lunch took a long time, so it was already after five in the afternoon when they returned to their homes.

"Well, here we are, at home," Nick said with some embarrassment, realizing he felt a growing attraction for Lory. "Thank you for your company!" he added, offering Lory a typical Italian style kiss on the cheek. Lory wasn't ready to admit, even to herself, that the touch of their faces made her feel a special vibration in her heart. At the time, she did not attribute any particular importance to this emotion. She only hoped to build a strong friendship with Nick. So, she thanked him for a nice day, turned on her heal, and went to her flat, her head refilling with swirling thoughts about the cultural programs of the upcoming week.

CHAPTER TWO

The Daily Routine

Soon, Lory added a new task to her already busy schedule: teaching art history to the Veltmann's son, Phil. Paul and Ingrid Veltmann were especially grateful to Lorain for this favor, so she figured the extra work provided some advantage for her, and it would have been awkward to deny a private request from the Director.

Phil was a diligent and intelligent young man, attending the last year of a comprehensive grammar school in Rome. Phil easily managed the challenge of not only learning Italian quickly but also applying it to his studies every day. He'd integrated into his Roman secondary school community quite well. Moreover, he demonstrated a special interest in arts, music, and history. So, according to her agreement with the Veltmanns, Lory led history and criticism of fine arts and music lessons three times a week. Phil had a serious look for his age. He was tall and athletic with short, red hair and wore rectangular glasses. In addition, when Lory did not feel the inclination to mingle at the receptions that followed Institute cultural events, Phil turned out to be a charming companion. During these events they spoke at length about the exhibited artworks and the styles of the artists, rather than more mundane topics.

The autumn passed quickly and Lory began to prepare the Christmas programs, the most important of the year both for the Institute and for Lory. Opening ceremonies followed by receptions at the Holland Institute attracted a wide array of the diplomatic and cultural personalities from the international community in Rome. Consequently, Lory felt that her first Christmas program must be unforgettable. The Christmas concert and the exhibition, which would remain open until spring, were chosen by her with the agreement of the Director. By then, Veltmann's approval of Lory's programs was mostly just a formality.

Lory decided on a Van Gogh exhibit, which she began to organize far in advance of the holidays. She contacted a number of prestigious institutions to secure the paintings on loan, including the Van Gogh Museum in Amsterdam, the Musee d'Orsay in Paris, the Art Gallery of Berlin and the Armand Hammer Museum of Art in Los Angeles. By the beginning of December, all documentation of transportation and insurance had to be ready to receive the paintings, which, except for the ones from Los Angeles, arrived to the duty free area in via Merulana, where in exchange of the right documents, Lory and Gigi, received them. Lory felt deep relief once all these artistic treasures were safely delivered. Next, she had to install the paintings in the gallery at the Institute. To ensure sufficient time to execute all this, she cancelled her weekend plans with Nick, who received the news with disappointment but understanding. In fact, Nick offered to help install the paintings. Lory was grateful for the help, which was badly needed considering that she only Gigi to assist with the physical work. It required two people to lift each heavy and extremely valuable painting. With Nick's help Lory could stand back and choose each painting's best position. They repeated the process of lifting and holding each painting in position for all twenty of the masterworks. Then Lory had to translate, print and affix labels with the details for each work of art to the wall next to it. Preparing the entire installation took more than a week of hard work.

Once installation was complete, Lory had to concentrate on her opening speech. Typically, she asked an art expert to briefly present the exhibited artworks and officially open the prestigious exhibition. Since most of the paintings for this exhibition were from the Museum d'Orsay, she decided to ask its Director, Mr. Laurence des Chavignon, to present the exhibit. Mr. Des Chavignon accepted with pleasure, looking forward to spending the Christmas holidays in Rome with his wife.

CHAPTER THREE

Christmas

As always, the time spent preparing for an event flew by. But now that the guests arrived, time slowed down, moving painfully slowly, never coming to an end, Lory thought while giving her opening speech.

However, the evening passed surprisingly smoothly, and Lory was extremely happy with the success of Mr. des Chavignon's presentation. After the opening ceremony, she made the obligatory rounds in the gallery and in the salon where the reception was being held. Throughout the event her gaze often met with Nick's and Phil's, helping her recharge. Beyond the opening ceremony, the exhibition itself was also a great success. The paintings included *The Potato Eaters* (1885), *The Langlois Bridge* (1887), *The Sower* (1888), *Sunflowers* (1889), *The Yellow House (The Street*, 1888), *The Bedroom* (1888), *Self-portrait as a Painter* (1887-88), *Wheatfield with a Reaper* (1889), *Almond Blossom* (1890), *Irises* (1890), *Wheatfield under Thunderclouds* (1890), *Wheatfield with Crows* (1890), *Tree Roots* (1890), *Vincent Van Gogh Painting Sunflowers* by Paul Gouguin (1888), then again from Van Gogh the *Autoportrait* (1889), *Chaumes de Cordeville* (1890), *Les Tournesols* (1888), *Alberi davanti all'ospizio di Saint-Paul* (1889), and finally the *Notte stellata sul Rodano* (1888). Most guests took the opportunity to return to admire Van Gogh's paintings multiple times. Although there were relatively few paintings on exhibit, the carefully curated, extremely valuable representation of Van Gogh's work made up for its size, fascinating the visitors.

After making the rounds Lory and Phil met up in a quiet corner of the salon, chatting with one another about nothing in particular. They stayed amicably together until all the guests left, many confirming their planned presence at the Christmas Eve concert the next day. Holiday events required a lot of focus, since every detail was important, beginning with security for the VIP guests, ensured through the indispensable safety measures of the Roman police, to the decorative lights at the entrance. The guest lists for such events was tightly controlled.

It was the same for the Christmas Eve concert the next day, for which Lory expected even more people. Being part of the official holiday events in Rome, the concert attracted not only members of the diplomatic corps and the usual art lovers, collectors and experts, but all those who wanted to take part in the holiday spirit. The Holland Institute had rented the Auditorium of Rome in the Parco della Musica for the event. Lory's extreme fatigue from all the time spent choosing the right musicians was not in vain. She selected the world famous Holland Symphonic Orchestra. Luckily, the New Year's Concert did not require so much attention and worry, since it took place in the smaller concert hall at the Institute with a more restricted circle of guests, and was to be performed by the Holland Chamber Orchestra, which was also very popular and enjoyed success worldwide.

She was thinking about these particulars while doing her make up and adding the final touches to her dress for the Christmas Eve concert. According to the official agreement, she had to arrive at the auditorium an hour before the concert to oversee both the arrangements and the musicians. Nick had kindly offered to drive her, and she was pleased to accept. The last thing she needed was the stress of Roman traffic while mentally practicing her introduction for the concert program. They arrived on time and the moment she stepped onto the stage to pronounce the first words of her speech, "Ladies and gentlemen, lovers of music..." all her worries disappeared. She began to speak calmly with a sense of great love and a desire to hold the world in an immense hug.

The concert program was extraordinary. In the first half, attendees enjoyed the *1-3 Harnoncourt* and the *Pastorale* from the *Christmas Oratorio* of J. S. Bach, the *Symphony of Christmas Carol* from the *Carol Symphony* of Victor Hely-Hutchinson, the *Christmas Tree* piano concerto for four hands of F. Liszt, then the *Waltz of the Flower* from the *Nutcracker* of Tchaikovsky. After that came an intermission, which Lory used to recharge over coffee with Nick.

"You know, I wonder where Phil could be. He promised to be here and give his support, but I haven't seen him in the audience. By any chance, have you seen him, Nick?"

"No, I haven't, but to be honest, I haven't been looking for him. Veltmann asked me to entertain the des Chavignon couple, since you had your hands full. To be honest, it was a nice surprise to lose them for a little while to be here with you. They went to the toilet and then wanted to have a drink – I figured they didn't require my company for that."

"Ha! Veltmann really takes the task of being a good host to extremes. I don't understand why we can't leave the des Chavignons alone, even if they are VIP guests, and let them enjoy a little freedom. For God's sake, they are highly-skilled, cosmopolitan people, not absent-minded professors, who can't be trusted to across the street without help!"

"Exactly. But what can we do? Anyway, now that I think about it, it is strange that I haven't seen Phil yet, having been with the Veltmanns and the des Chavignons the whole time." Nick looked up and then he stood up. "Sorry, but I have to leave you. I see them heading toward their seats. Anyway, I'll get to drive you home, right? I'm pretty sure they can drive back without me. Now, I must complete my very important job, for which I have you to thank you."

"All right. Ciao. See you after the concert!" Lory answered and they both returned to their seats.

The second half of the concert proved unforgettable and was an absolute success with its extraordinary program, which included: the *In Terra Pax* from Gerald Finzi, the *Quem Vidist Pastores* from Francis Poulenc, the *Weihnachtmusik* from Arnold Shoenberg, the *A Ceremony of Carols* from Benjamin Britten and at the end the *Shepherds farewell* of *The Childhood of Christ* from Hector Berlioz.

When the concert ended, Lory and Nick waited for Veltmann to congratulation to Conductor, Maestro Jan Willem de Vriend, after which the musicians got on a bus to return to their accommodations at the Hotel Pamphili in Via Aurela Antica. The musicians seemed very satisfied with their accommodations, a five-star sport and wellness hotel located at the top of Gianicolo hill, from where they could enjoy a particularly captivating view of the Eternal City.

"Finally! It's about time that's over," Lory sighed, sitting beside Nick in the car, giving her tired soles a massage.

"You should be proud of yourself. Both of your events were great successes, both the exhibit opening yesterday and the concert this evening. Now your only remaining task is to accompany the des Chavignons, tomorrow, to keep Veltmann satisfied."

"Right. Tomorrow I'll take them on a sight-seeing tour around the historical center and accompany them to the Veltmanns for dinner. Will you be there?"

"What a question! Of course not! These guests belong to your discipline not to mine one. Why would Veltmann invite the Scientific Secretary to a dinner for the guests of an artistic event? But don't worry, I will survive."

"I'm sure you will, lucky you. By the way, are your parents coming to visit for the holidays? Mine arrive tomorrow evening. Because of the dinner, I asked Veltmann if Antonio could pick them up at the airport. It's not every day they get to be driven by an official driver. I think they'll be impressed and touched by the gesture."

"Congrats to you! You're such a great planner. I could have pick them up, since my parents are arriving on the same flight. But to travel in Rome with an official driver is surely much more elegant. Anyway, here we are. Welcome back to the Institute! Merry Christmas and enjoy the sightseeing tour tomorrow. Bye."

"Merry Christmas to you, too, and thank you for everything. Good night!" Lory blew a quick airy kiss to Nick's face and hurried out of the car. By the time Nick came to his sense, he could only see her silhouette flying into her flat.

December 25th, Christmas Day, arrived. According to the agreement with des Chavignons, Lory met them after breakfast to take them sightseeing. But, when she arrived, Laurence des Chavignon made a special request. "Dear Lorain, would you do us the favor of letting us into the gallery to admire the exhibition one more time? We simply can't take our eyes off these masterpieces."

"Of course. Just a minute and while I get the key and turn off the security." Lory turned on her heel and hurried to the reception area locating the key from a board that held a spare key for every room of the Institute.

When they entered the gallery, they were stunned by what they saw: three of the Van Goghs were no longer on the wall. They had disappeared.

"How is this possible? Where can they be?" Lory exclaimed.

"For God's sake! These paintings are worth a fortune!" Laurence des Chavignon cried out.

"Please do not touch anything and leave the gallery. I will call the police immediately!" Lory ran like down the hall with the speed of thunder to alert the whole Institute.

Lory's Institute colleagues gathered quickly in front of the gallery door and began to debate the efficiency of their safety measures. The police arrived quickly to investigate. Captain Luigi Ferretti led the interrogation of Institute staff in the reading room of the Institute's library, starting with Lory.

"Please tell me which paintings disappeared and exactly what you saw when you were last in the gallery, prior to opening the doors this morning."

"Well, three Van Gogh paintings disappeared: the *Sunflowers*, the *Yellow House* and the *Self-Portrait as a Painter*," Lory began. "The last time I was in the gallery was the day before yesterday, on the 23rd, at about midnight or so. Since that time, I haven't had a minute to go back into the gallery because of I was in charge of managing the Christmas Eve concert in the auditorium at the

Parco della Musica. When I entered the gallery this morning I had a strange feeling, as if someone was there, in addition to me and the des Chavignons. But when I ran around the gallery to identify which paintings were missing, I didn't see anyone else."

"Thank you Dottoressa Henness. If you happen to remember anything that seems strange in relation to the robbery, even if it seems insignificant, please let me know. We will inform you about every step of the investigation as we continue. Furthermore, I probably don't need to mention this, but nobody who stayed at the Institute yesterday night can leave Rome, even temporarily. Would you please provide a list of all the participants of the opening ceremony for the exhibit."

"Yes, of course I will," Lory responded. She stood and went directly to her office to satisfy the captain's request.

Captain Ferretti completed his questioning of the staff and des Chavignons, without gaining much useful information. Nobody saw or heard anything strange during the opening ceremony or the following day. The policy had nothing to go on. Veltmann was beside himself, standing in front of the library with the des Chavignons and other colleagues talking about insurance for the paintings.

"The good news is that we will likely get an additional detective from the insurance company. By the way, which insurance company did you contract with, Miss Hennes?" des Chavignon asked Lory.

"With Generali, sir. I have already informed them about the robbery and they said they would send an inspector to us in spite of it being the holidays.

"Who knows when we will be given permission to go home?" complained Madame des Chavignon.

"Don't worry my dear. As soon they rule us out as suspects we can go home. Then we will only have to be available in case of necessity."

"Oh, Monsieur des Chavignon, as the Director of the Museum d'Orsay you must be above every suspicion!" Lorain added respectfully.

"Thank you, you are very kind. But, we can only be removed from the list of suspects if we have an incontestable alibi. I told the Captain that on the 23rd we participated in the exhibition's opening ceremony, after which we spent the night in the Institute's guest apartment. During the whole day of the 24th we travelled around Rome with the Veltmanns and in the evening we were present at the concert."

At that moment the library door opened and Captain Ferretti headed straight for Lory.

"Dottoressa Hennes, would you please show me the gallery's security system? It is very probable that the thief had access to the Institute's keys and knew the password for the alarm system, too."

"Of course! Please follow me Captain Ferretti and I will show you how the alarm system works." Lory led Captain Ferretti to the reception area. "Well, as you can see," Lory started to explain, "the alarm system is based on a net of lasers activated throughout the gallery when it is closed. In addition, there are some security cameras fixed on the gallery walls connected to screens in the reception area that record every event and movement in the gallery, day and night. The Receptionist can also monitor everything that happens in the gallery. In addition, at the exhibit opening ceremony, you and the police were present at the Institute's front gate, and, as always, our Secretary was at the entrance greeting and confirming every guest. She knows everybody personally, so it's not likely anyone got past her, though, of course, it is not impossible."

"Let's review. So, during the opening ceremony and reception on the 23rd Umberto Bianchetti, the Receptionist, and Gianluigi Colombari, the Caretaker, were on duty, observing movements at the entrance and in the gallery," Captain Ferretti summarized, "and after the event you closed the door of the gallery and activated the alarm system personally."

"That's right."

"Are there any security cameras on the external walls of the Institute, in addition to those in the gallery?"

“Yes.”

“Then hopefully the film recorded on the night in question is still available. I’d like to see it as soon as possible.”

“Of course,” Lory answered.

“Then, during the day of the 24th the gallery was closed and not scheduled to reopen until Thursday the 27th.”

“Precisely. I may have forgotten to mention that during the opening ceremony and reception on the 23rd we set up a cloakroom in the niche behind the reception area. The Caretaker’s daughter Isabella, and one of her classmates where were on duty, happy for a little extra work and income before the holidays.”

“All right, I see. No one could hide in the cloakroom unless they knew about it and the thief couldn’t be a stranger because he or she must have known the alarm system code.”

“Which he or she reactivated after the robbery, since this morning when I grabbed the key I turned off the alarm system myself to let the des Chavignons into the gallery.”

“This is an exceptional case. Very interesting.” Captain Ferretti stated, frustrated. “Well, thank you, Dottoressa Hennes. That is all for now. I will contact you when we know more. And please, if any overlooked detail comes to mind, call me! Good-bye.”

“Of course, I will Captain Ferretti! Bye-bye.”

It was already a half past noon when the investigation concluded and the police left, so Lory had to act quickly to ask her parents not to come to see her. Their presence at the Institute would have complicated the situation and, with the ongoing investigation, Lory did not think she would have enough time to spend with them.

“Don’t worry my dear! We understand,” her mother responded on the phone. “The investigation must take precedence. We can meet after this storm passes, when the thief has been caught.”

“Thank you so much for understanding, mom. I am so sorry!”

“I know, my love, we are sorry, too, especially for the robbery! Just stay focused and give your full support to the police. Go now, I don’t want to take up any more of your time.”

“All right. Thank you again. I will call soon. Hugs and kisses!”

"Hugs and kisses! Good-bye dear."

At last, Lory could spend some time alone to put her thoughts in order. So much had happened in the last two days! She poured herself a whisky and sat down in a cozy armchair in her flat to think it all over. Sitting there, she suddenly remembered asking Nick during intermission about Phil's absence.

"I hope he has nothing to do with the robbery," she said to herself. "He doesn't use drugs or gamble at the casinos," she thought, "so it's likely he needs that kind of money." But where had he been during the concert and all day long on the 24th? In fact, he hadn't even appeared during the investigation. Lory decided to find out where Phil had been before mentioning his absence to Captain Ferretti. Just as she decided to follow up, the Institute's internal phoneline started ringing.

"Hello!" Lory answered picking up the receiver.

"Good evening Dottoressa. This is Gigi. Sorry for disturbing you so late, but Antonio is wondering if he should go to the airport to pick up your parents."

"Oh, thank you so much for calling Gigi. I am so sorry, but I forgot to tell Antonio that my parents aren't coming. Please tell him that I thank him, but there's no need for his service."

"All right Dottoressa, I will tell him."

"By the way Gigi," Lory continued, "If you have a minute, I have a question."

"Yes, of course, just ask, Dottoressa!"

"You're the one who provided Captain Ferretti with the names of the people working and staying at the Institute, right?"

"Yes. "

"Can you tell me what you told to the police about Mr. Philip's absence?"

"Of course. According to the Director, Mr. Philip spent the 24th at his girlfriend's and returned only this afternoon."

"Thank you Gigi. That's very good news. Then the Captain will talk to him later."

"Yes, that's what he said."

"Thank you again, and Merry Christmas!"

"Thank you! And the same to you, Dottoressa!"

Lory sat back in her armchair with a deep sigh of relief. "So," she thought, "Phil has a girlfriend and he never even mentioned her. But that's irrelevant right now. The most important thing is that he has an irrefutable alibi." Just as she began to think back on the happenings of the day, the phone rang again.

"Hello!" Lory answered.

"Hi, Lory!"

"Hi Nick! What's new? Did you go pick up your parents at the airport?"

"Well, no. They postponed their visit because of the robbery."

"So did mine."

"Hey, so what are you doing? You see, I was just getting ready to prepare dinner and thought maybe you could come join me so we could have dinner together and talk over all of today's happenings. What do you think?"

"Yes, that would be excellent! Thank you. I'll be there."

"Great! Dinner's at six, so come on over in an hour or sooner, if you like."

"All right! Should I bring anything?"

"Nothing, just yourself. But please don't be late, I'm making spaghetti, which is best eaten while it's still warm."

"I'll be there at six sharp! That'll give me time to take a shower. See you soon. Bye." She put down the receiver, took off her clothes and found herself skipping to the shower.

She arrived at Nick's exactly on time.

"I brought a bottle of wine. It's a good thing that I always keep a few bottles at home, isn't it? It's white. I hope that works."

"Wow! You are punctual and beautiful. White wine is excellent because dinner is spaghetti alle vongole veraci, your favorite,if I remember correctly."

"How..."

"...could I get the vongole? This afternoon, after I told my parents about the robbery and they deciding not to come, I had a little free time, so I went to the fish market in Fiumicino."

"Wow, you're fantastic!"

"Aren't I? And, dinner is served Madam! So please take your seat."

"It's about time I ate something. Today was so busy, I didn't even have lunch."

"Here you are. You can eat a double portion to make up for it – there's plenty of food. I'll open the wine. Wow, a Sardinian Vermentino!"

The evening at Nick's was perfect, although, they couldn't come up with any additional important details, despite going over the robbery again and again. In the end, they concluded that they had nothing new to offer Captain Ferretti.

"Well, the facts that we know lead nowhere!" Lory exclaimed. "We don't have enough information. It doesn't make sense to keep going over it hoping something pops up. And it's very late. Time to go to bed." She stood up and headed to the door.

"Sadly, I have to agree with you. But at least it's clear that without someone helping from the inside, it was impossible to commit this crime," Nick said accompanying Lory to the door.

"Yes, that is true. Well, thank you for the dinner. It was magnificent!"

"You are welcome. It was my pleasure."

"Good night Nick. See you tomorrow."

"The same to you, and sweet dreams. Bye."

Lory started the next day in Veltmann's office, because the Generali Insurance Company Inspector had arrived. Before entering Veltmann's office, she thought how grateful she was that the previous evening she and Nick had analyzed the facts about the robbery in great detail. Now, she felt well prepared to give the Inspector a detailed picture of the crime.

"Inspector Pavoni, please meet Dottoressa Lorain Hennes, our Artistic Secretary."

"Nice to meet you Dottoressa Hennes!"

"Dottoressa, this is Mr. Luciano Pavoni, the Inspector from Generali."

"Nice to meet you, Inspector Pavoni. We are at your service," Lory responded politely.

"Thank you. I was told that, after Mr. Veltmann, of course, you are the most important person in connection with the robbery, since it is in connection with paintings that disappeared from the exhibit you organized."

"Yes. That's right."

"Well, then I will not take any more of Mr. Veltmann's precious time, if you, Dottoressa, can show me the scene of the robbery and explain the facts we know about the circumstances."

"Certainly, just follow me, please," Lory answered standing up immediately, ready to act.

"Ispettore, thank you for your availability in spite of the holidays," said Veltmann shaking Inspector Pavoni's hand.

"It is my duty. Thank you for your time Direttore. Good-bye."

"Bye-bye!"

Lory led Inspector Pavoni to the reception area, explaining, "I think I should show you how exactly we discovered the robbery. So, let's start at the reception area where on the morning of the 25th I turned off the alarm system and grabbed the key to let the des Chavignons into the gallery."

"Perfect! Dottoressa, you think like an inspector."

"Thank you, I'm trying. So, here we are. Let me introduce you to Mr. Umberto Bianchetti, our Receptionist. Umberto, this is Mr. Luciano Pavoni, the official Inspector from the Generali Insurance Company," Lory introduced Umberto to the Inspector.

"Nice to meet you! What can I do for you, Inspector?" Umberto responded.

"Nice to meet you, too. Let's start with the alarm system. Can you explain to me how exactly it works? I would also like to know where you during the time period established by the police, between 24:15 on the 23rd and 08:30 on the 25th, the moment of the discovery of the robbery. Is that right, Dottoressa Hennes?"

"Yes, exactly. We are all aware of how the alarm system functions, but the code is secret, so I keep it on my computer. Except for me it is known by only you Mr. Pavoni."

"All right. Then let's proceed, step by step!"

Lory spent the whole morning with Inspector Pavoni, explaining all she knew about the crime in great detail. He also questioned the same employees, families and guests of the Institute that Captain Ferretti had. Finally, he scheduled an appointment with Captain Ferretti and Lory at three in the afternoon.

"While waiting for our appointment with Captain Ferretti, let me invite you for a working lunch, Dottoressa Hennes."

"With pleasure. Thank you. I know a good restaurant near the Institute," Lory responded, politely, accepting that this Christmas would be completely cancelled from her life.

"Great! To be honest, I hoped you'd have an excellent recommendation."

The lunch with the inspector went better than Lory had expected. She had to acknowledge that Pavoni was far less unpleasant than she had thought at the first sight.

The police station for foreigners in Rome is located at the top of Quirinalis Hill, opposite the entrance to the Quirinalis Palace. Pavoni knew the city quite well and drove well, too. Since Saint Steven's Day is observe on the 26th, Roman traffic was light. They drove around the Villa Borghese to reach Via XX Settembre, which led them directly to Quirinalis Square. Captain Ferretti had informed the Receptionist of their planned arrival. A policeman was waiting to accompany them to the Captain's office. After introductions were made, they took their seats and reviewed the facts and the unknowns about the robbery, while policemen were occasionally called into the office to receive orders in connection with the investigation. Lory and Captain Pavoni learned that an examination of the bank accounts of all Holland Institute employees conducted by the Italian police uncovered a lump sum of 200,000 euros that had been transferred to Daniel Prick's account the day before.

"How long has Mr. Prick been working for the Holland Institute?" Captain Ferretti asked Lory.

"He arrived two years before me, so this is his third year in Rome. But he has always worked for Dutch Ministry of Foreign Affairs."

"Could he have had access to the alarm system code?" Captain Pavoni asked, closing in on Prick.

"Well, it would be challenging, but it is not impossible. He's the one person who can enter any office unobserved. He's known for his ongoing research into our invoices and bills.

"Although I protect the security code with a password, Mr. Prick could have discovered it. He is said to be the best computer expert in the Ministry with excellent decoding abilities."

"That's it! Clearly he's our suspect," responded the Captain Ferretti. "All that remains is to figure out who his accomplices were."

"And how will we do that?" Lory asked timidly, sitting between two sleuths on the scent.

"You must not show any sign that we suspect him. The safer Prick feels, the better," explained Captain Ferretti. "We are going to contact the Dutch Police. We are also examining the recent transactions of Italian art dealers. We have moles in that micro-society, so you can be assured that we will catch him, if he sold the paintings in Italy, which is the most obvious way to get rid of them as soon as possible."

"All right." Lory nodded repeatedly comprehending her role. She felt a sense of calm starting to spread through her, based on the words of the Captain, as she started to relax after two days and nights nonstop worry. "Do you think the paintings can be still found?" she asked, daring to let a little hope into her voice.

"Since the theft occurred so recently, we have a good chance of it. In our experience with stolen artwork, it is easiest to reclaim the pieces if we can move quickly, within the first week. But, to be honest, there have been cases where we found such works only years after the crime, using the catalog of missing objects," Captain Pavoni summed up the situation.

"We may have an advantage, in that Prick seems new to the world of crime," added Captain Ferretti. "Otherwise, he would have transferred the proceeds from the paintings to a secret bank account."

"It is late, Dottoressa, and it's time we return you to the Institute. From now on you must leave everything to us. Just remember to act naturally as we proceed."

"I will. Thank you." Lory responded with renewed confidence.

"I'll give you a ride back." So, they said farewell to Captain Ferretti in order to move ahead with the strategy they just agree upon.

CHAPTER FOUR

The exposure

Thursday morning, after the Christmas holidays, Lory woke up at her normal time for work. She had slept well, but was quite concerned about being able to act natural with her colleagues, as she promised the Captains. She was especially annoyed to have to keep the secret from Nick. But, she had no choice but to keep the latest results of the investigation to herself. So, she tried to behave as normally as possible.

At work, the first person she met, luckily, was Veltmann, who didn't notice the somewhat unnatural smile on her face when she wished him good morning. She would need to work on acting more natural before running into Prick. She decided to stay in her office till noon, and managed arrangements to close the Institute and Gallery mostly by phone, except for when she asked Umberto to hang the "Closed" sign on the main entrance and asked Gigi to help her obtain a new code for the alarm system. She also informed Veltmann that the police had agreed that the des Chavignons could leave Rome to return to Paris. Veltmann was happy with the news and asked Lory about her meeting with the two inspectors at the police station. Lory managed to politely avoid giving away any information. She changed the subject to Phil, whose education she wanted to continue. At first Veltmann hesitated a bit, saying it was too early to restart his son's instruction with the ongoing investigation, but then realized that that this activity had no bearing on the police work. He agreed with Lory and promised to send Phil to her office after school around four o'clock in the afternoon.

"Hi Lory! May I come in." Phil arrived right on time.

"Hi! Of course."

"What happened is horrible. I heard the news right after I returned from Anna's. Do the police know anything more?"

"No. Nothing," Lory lied. "They are going around in circles. But let's change topics. What about you? I didn't know you had such a serious relationship with a girl that you spent the Christmas with her family."

"Well, yes. We've been together for three months. But my parents are not happy about it, because they find Anna's family too conservative and religious. To be honest they really are religious. I'd never been to so many church services, until I met Anna. I was surprised my parents accepted my decision to spend this Christmas with Anna and her family. I'd like to get engaged, but that would seem rushed to both her parents and mine."

"Oh, that's wonderful. But you have all the time you need to make such an important decision. In the meantime, you can get to know each other better, and you will see, if she really is the one. The more you wait, the more your love will grow."

"I know you are right, or I at least I hope so."

"Anyways, let's start our lesson. After the Romanesque style we arrive to the Gothic, of which there are hardly any examples in Rome."

They continued with their lesson till six o'clock without any breaks, virtually visiting the most beautiful, impressive, and famous Gothic churches of Europe. Then they said farewell and agreed on the next lesson for tomorrow. By then, there was no one in the office except Lory. Being alone, she began to play with the idea of conducting her own investigation in her colleagues' offices, when her external line started ringing. It was Captain Ferretti speaking.

"I am glad to find you still in the office! I just call to inform that we believe the Dutch mafia was behind the robbery with an Italian accomplice with an art dealership in Florence. That's all I can tell you for now. Tomorrow, I will come to your office at eight a.m. and let you know more details. Our 'friend' doesn't suspect anything, does he?"

"Wow! Everything here fine. Except for me, nobody knows anything."

"We will use the pretext of examining your computer and that of the Caretaker to discover how the robber got the alarm system's code. I will explain the rest tomorrow. Good-bye."

"Bye-bye and have a nice evening. I will see you tomorrow," Lory responded with a deep sense of relief. Feeling much calmer, she had a light dinner and went to bed early.

The next morning, she woke up very early. She was too excited to sleep any longer. She got up, dressed in hurry and went to the office, where she found no one, of course. She couldn't do any serious work as she tried to figure out how captain Ferretti had found the connection to the Dutch mafia and their Italian accomplice. Eventually, she heard the arrival of her colleagues, talking to one another in the corridor. Then, Captain Ferretti arrived with two computer experts from the police department and Captain Pavoni. They went directly to Lory's office and, according to their secret plan, began to examine her computer. Out of curiosity, Prick appeared at the open door to Lory's office. When captain Ferretti told him that they would come to his office soon, he retired quickly, seeming a bit disturbed but without any noticeable suspicion. Then Captain Ferretti asked Lory to call the Director to join them in her office so that he could share the latest results of the investigation with both of them at the same time. Veltmann came immediately and was stunned by the news.

"Mr. Veltmann, I regret to have to inform you that your security camera recorded a car in front of the Institute's gate, with its Italian registration number visible. The camera also recorded several individuals bringing three paintings out of the Institute and loading them into the car. In addition, your accountant, Mr. Daniel Prick, is clearly visible on the recording, waving to the driver of the car in question and then going back into the Institute closing the gate. His guilt is further proved by the fact that on the 25th of December, the tidy sum of 200,000 euro was transferred to his bank account. At this point, I kindly request that you come with me to Mr. Prick's office."

"This is both horrible and absolutely incredible. Of course, I will take you to Mr. Prick's office. Please follow me."

As they entered the Accountant's office, Daniel Prick showed signs of nervousness, which increased as Captain Ferretti began the usual police line: "Dottore Daniel Prick, I arrest you on the basis of the charge of the robbery of three Van Gogh paintings from the gallery of the Holland Institute on the night of the 24th of December. I remind you of your right to remain silent. Everything you say can be used against you." One of the officers handcuffed Prick. "You can take him away. Now, Mr. Veltmann, I would like to talk with you."

"All right. But let's go to my office where we can have more space," the Director responded, still pale with the shock of the morning's events.

Captain Ferretti began talking as soon as they entered the Director's office. "I have good news for you. The paintings were found in the art shop of Prick's Italian accomplice in Florence. They can be returned to be put back in place on your gallery wall later today."

"That's amazing!" Lory cried with excitement. "I'm sorry, but I was so stressed because I felt responsible for their disappearance."

"Congratulation Captain! This is an excellent work!" Veltmann joined Lory's excitement.

"And let me congratulate you, too, Captain Ferretti! I have to admit the Roman police were very effective," added Pavoni. "Therefore, all I have to do is wait for the paintings' return to confirm their authenticity. Then I can declare the case is solved and close the investigation, closing any insurance claims."

"Dear Sirs and Dottoressa," continued Captain Ferretti standing up. "Thank you for your kind availability and cooperation with us. I wish you all the best for the New Year!"

"We thank you, too," added Veltmann, vigorously shaking the Captain's hand, "and we also wish you a Happy New Year!"

"Good-bye! Hopefully we will meet again, but not because of another crime!"

"Oh, yes…if you'd like, we can add your name to our guest list, as well as those of your colleagues, and of course, your name as well, Mr. Pavoni. That way we will have more joyful occasions to meet each other at future cultural events."

"How nice of you! Thank you. We will look forward to attending your events with pleasure, won't we Mr. Pavoni?"

"Certainly! I will look forward to joining Captain Ferretti, as a regular guest with pleasure."

"I'm happy to hear that! We look forward to seeing you at your next event. Good-bye!" And with that, Captain Ferretti left the Institute.

Lory and Captain Pavoni waited together for the return of the stolen paintings, which arrived soon, transported by an armored police car. At the same time, an art expert arrived to confirm the authenticity of the paintings. Once he had examined and certified them, the paintings were put back in their places in the gallery within the hour. Pavoni and the expert, satisfied with the results of their work, said good-bye and left the Institute, too. Lory remained for a while in the gallery, gazing at the returned masterpieces. Then she went to Veltmann's office to inform him about their return.

"You know, Dottoressa Hennes, you have again demonstrated your professionalism. I believe you are qualified for a higher position than the one you hold. I congratulate you for the successful conclusion of this incident."

"Thank you, Sir, you flatter me."

"Don't be so shy. You kept every detail of the case under control and you managed to avoid panic. You calmed your colleagues and helped them face what seemed like a hopeless situation. On another note, I'd like discuss our lost Christmas. My wife and I would like to invite all the Institute staff with their spouse for a make-up Christmas dinner at our residence this evening. Would you please inform everyone? Dinner will start at six o'clock. And please tell them not to bring any Christmas presents."

"Sir, that's a great idea and a wonderful gesture on your part! Of course, I will invite everybody. If that is all, I'll take care of it right away."

"Perfect. See you this evening." Veltmann ended the discussion and Lory left her office in a hurry to contact the staff.

CHAPTER FIVE

Christmas Revisited

On the evening of the 29th, the Institute's staff and their spouses gathered at the residence, except, of course, for Daniel Prick, who was travelling back to the Netherlands with his accomplices in police custody to face justice. The Veltmanns did their best to organize a perfect Christmas party, charging their chef with the preparation of multiple courses for the dinner. They also employed waitresses so that the guests could relax and enjoy one another's company. The guests arrived wearing their best evening wear. Veltmann offered a toast in welcome, creating a celebratory atmosphere that lasted all the evening long.

"Dear colleagues and friends, we have had a difficult week. Several Dutch masterpieces and our Christmas were stolen. Consequently, I believe we all deserve to celebrate both a belated Christmas and the return of the Van Gogh's to our gallery. So, let's drink to this honest, conscientious and loyal community, which it is a great pleasure to lead! Let's clink our glasses to Christmas of 2012 and I invite all of you to enjoy the artistry of our chef! I wish you all a Merry Christmas!"

"Merry Christmas!" replied the guests, happy to reclaim their lost Christmas.

Lory was seated to the right of Veltmann, who occupied the head of the table. Nick was seated across from her. Ingrid sat at the other end, facing her husband, engaging the guests at that half of the table. Gigi sat next to Lory and across from him, Julienne Becker, who took her seat next to Nick. Umberto Bianchetti, sat next to her. Perla Colombari sat opposite Umberto, with Antonio next to her. Next to him, Elisabetta Bianchetti was sitting according to the seating cards, and across from her, next to Umberto, Laura Rotondo, beside whom sat Peter Becker, Julienne's husband.

As they enjoyed their magnificent dinner. Conversation was congenially, although somewhat restrained, considering the formality of the event. Then they retired to the salon for coffee and whisky.

Lory was finally able to tell Nick the whole story of the investigation with all of its complexity. Veltmann informed everybody of the result of the investigation and the fact that after reporting the details of the crime to the Dutch Ministry of Culture, he asked for a new accountant to replace Prick. Then he invited his guests to the New Year's ball he and Ingrid were hosting at their residence. At that point, Phil, Anna and Isabella joined the party, put on some CDs and and invited everybody to dance. Nick asked Lory to dance with him and she accepted without hesitation. At first they both felt somewhat awkward, but after a few minutes spent talking about Phil and Anna's relationship, they clung together with undeniable attraction. By the waltz, they were dancing as if they had always danced together.

Since the Institute was closed for the weekend, they could all relax more freely, drinking and dancing. Since everyone, except Anna, lived at the Institute, Phil, at Nick's suggestion, asked Lory if Anna could stay in her flat, so no one had to drive later. Lory agreed with pleasure. The party ended after midnight, when the guests said good night their hosts and to one another. Lory phoned Anna's parents to tell them their daughter would spend the night with her and took Anna to her flat. She provided a towel, pajamas and a toothbrush. While Anna was in the bathroom she prepared the spare bedroom for her. They were both too very tired to stay up chatting, so, after a short shower each went to bed and fell asleep immediately. Exhausted by the events of the previous week, Lory slept till 10, when she was awakened by the heavenly smell of fresh coffee. She put her robe on quickly and went to the kitchen where she found Anna preparing breakfast.

"Good morning Dottoressa Lorain! I hope it's OK that I prepared a light breakfast. Your kitchen is very well equipped, so it's a great pleasure to cook in it."

"Good morning! And, please, call me Lorain! OK?"

"All right. I will try to to remember. I've made the bed and I put the sheets into the bathroom. Is that OK?"

"Oh, yes excellent, but you shouldn't have done it, I always do that for my guests."

"I just didn't want to be a bother."

"It's very nice of you, and it's a pleasure to help one's friends."

"You have a lovely personality. Phil said so, and now I see what he means."

"You are too kind. Well, let's have this magnificent breakfast. It smells so good that I might die of hunger, if we don't start eating at once!"

As they finished their breakfast, the phone rang. It was Phil, asking how they were doing, and if he could come to join them. They asked him to give them half an hour, just enough time for Lory to get dressed.

When Phil popped in, he greeted the two girls with a dazzling smile and offered an idea for how to spend the day. "I thought we could pass today together. I have a plan. Since Anna wants to be a zoologist, and we are located at the entrance of Villa Borghese, we could go to visit the "Bio-Park," the Roman zoo, together."

"What a great idea!" Lory answered spontaneously. "I haven't been there yet. Anna, do you really want to be a zoologist?"

"Yes, it's true and it's a fantastic idea, Phil. But I don't want to force you to come with us, Lorain, if you would rather not."

"I'd love to go. What about inviting Nick to come with us?" Lory suggested, thinking of her friend and dancing partner with personal interest.

"That's an excellent idea!" Phil answered. "I should have thought of it."

"That works for me, too!" Anna nodded enthusiastically.

"I'll give him a call," Lory said, "and in the meantime you can have a breakfast, Phil. We have coffee and everything else. Anna would you help him and make sure he eats!"

Anna and Phil went to the kitchen and Lory picked up the receiver to call Nick. Nick answered with a sleepy voice, "Hello."

"Good morning! It's Lory. Are you sleeping in?"

"Hi. What's up? Well, yes maybe I am. I just got up two minutes ago and I might go back to bed after your call."

"What a slug-a-bed! Forget about going back to bed! You have a half hour to get ready and join us for breakfast."

"What's the hurry? And what do you mean, 'us'? And why should I have breakfast with you?"

"Don't remember? It was your idea for Anna to stay and spend the night in my flat. So, we are here with Phil, and the youngsters would like to go to the Villa Borghese, to the Zoo, the so-called 'Bio-Park', with us, therefore, also with you. You know, Anna wants to be a zoologist, and could be an expert guide. Please don't say no!"

"What? An expert guide to the Bio what?"

"Bio-Park, the new name for the Roman Zoo here in the Borghese."

"I haven't been to the Roman Zoo yet," stuttered Nick.

"Then it's the perfect occasion. It will be a great fun! Don't make me beg, just get ready! But hurry up!" Lory put down the receiver without waiting for Nick's answer.

Then she rushed back to the kitchen to inform Anna and Phil that Nick would be joining them.

Nick arrived in less than 20 minutes. Lory left the door open, so the pleasant smell of fresh coffee led him directly into the kitchen where he found the excited trio.

They had a great time together at the Bio-Park. Lory, Nick, and Phil were an excellent audience for Anna's "professional" presentation, providing the perfect occasion for Anna to practice lecturing about animal science. After the Bio-Park, they went out for pizza together, joking and laughing throughout lunch. It was a pleasant way to end a fabulous day spent in such lovely company. In the middle of the afternoon, Lory and the two guys dropped Anna off at home.

CHAPTER SIX

Preparations for New Year's Eve and the Ball

After an easy Saturday spent with Anna and Phil, Lory and Nick decided to go shopping. Since most shops were closed for the holidays, they decided to go to Lory's favorite shopping center, the La Romanina Centro Commerciale. They started in the supermarket. After putting their purchases into the car, they returned to the center to look at the exclusive shops and boutiques. Walking side by side, Lory found it pleasant to be beside Nick. She felt a strange whisper in her soul, loud enough that she worried Nick could hear it, too. But fortunately, he showed no signs, except for saying he had a great time shopping with Lory and that they should do it more often. He added that it was more economical for them to go together, sharing one car. Lory couldn't help smiling and nodded, confirming her agreement. They each had a slice of pizza so they could shop without suffering pangs of hunger and then walked back to the car with magazines and the other things they bought.

Getting in the car, relaxed and satisfied, they decided to make shopping a regular outing on Saturdays, or at least every other Saturday. Sitting beside Nick in the car, Lory had the same feeling of being at home with him. While they were unpacking the trunk, Nick's hand touched hers and she felt an electric spark throughout her whole body. She was sure now that she wanted something more than friendship from Nick, but at the same time, the idea frightened her. With all these thoughts distracting, she said goodbye to Nick with much enthusiasm. He didn't think much about it, assuming that she was too tired to express much emotion. Thanking her again for the shopping trip, he said farewell and left her to rest.

But, instead of taking a nap, Lory went to the reception area, turned off the alarm system and checked to see if everything was all right in the gallery. She was returned to reality by Umberto's voice.

"Well, Dottoressa, you don't really think that the same crime can happen twice in one week!"

"Hi Umberto. You can never know. The last burglary could have been a distraction from a bigger one. But I see that everything is all right, so come with me and we can turn the alarm system back on."

Guiding Umberto out of the gallery she added, "It's better that everybody know that I check the gallery at different times every day."

"That's right, Dottoressa. The Director ordered me here at reception because we have to be on duty during the holidays."

"It's an excellent idea. I have to support it, although I hope that you will be compensated by the Institute for your sacrifice, Umberto?"

"I do it with pleasure Dottoressa." Lory smiled back at him.

"Now I have to go, Umberto. I still have a lot to do." Lory left the reception area for her flat.

The last day of the year began as an average one. Lory was happy that there was nothing to worry her at the end of what had been a successful year. The thought that the robbery could have ended her mission in Rome in failure still upset her. She tried to think of other things to get into the spirit of New Year's Eve and busied herself preparing for the ball. Being a typical Monday, shops were open, so she called her hairdresser for an appointment and spread her evening dresses on her bed to make her choice. She had just tried one on when the phone rang.

"Hello," Lory answered.

"Hi, my Sweet!"

"Hi Mom! How nice to hear your voice! Did you receive my message?"

"Yes Dear. We are so happy that the paintings were found! How are you? How are you spending New Year's Eve?"

"Thanks Mom. I am fine, now. I had was very worried about the stolen paintings, but now everything is all right. Tonight, the Veltmanns are hosting a ball for all the employees and their spouses, as well as some of their friends."

"I'm so glad everything ended well! My dear, there is something I need to tell you. Greg came to see us and asked for you. I told him that you were on a mission in Rome. Is that OK? I hope you don't mind."

"Greg's returned home and is looking for me? Are his parents still in Japan?"

"Yes dear, they are and Greg will return for another year to work on his PhD there. But while he is here on holiday, he wanted to visit you. I couldn't convince him not to do so. He said he would take the first flight he could get to Rome."

"Here? To me? When?

"I don't know, honey! I haven't the faintest idea. I am so sorry!"

"Don't worry Mom! It's not your fault!"

"Thank you, my sweet, for saying so, but if I had not talk to him about your mission…"

"Don't worry mom. I've got a call on the other line. Hold on if you can." Lory switched to the internal line. "Hello?"

"Hello Dottoressa. It's me, Umberto, at reception. There is a man from the Netherlands here looking for you."

"What? Here? What's his name?"

"Yes Dottoressa. He is standing in front of me and says his name is Gregory Bellmont."

"Good Heaven! Please tell him I will be there in a minute!" Lory switched lines. "Mom are you still there?"

"Yes my dear."

"Imagine! Greg has already arrived in Rome and he is here at the reception desk. I need to go talk to him. I'll call you this evening! Hugs and kisses, mom!"

"All right! Kisses! Bye-bye!"

Lory changed into a pair of jeans and a tee shirt and hurried to the reception area.

"How the hell did you get here, Greg?"

"Hi Lory! It is so nice to see you!"

"Yes. Sorry. It's nice to see you, too, but it's such a surprise!"

"I was surprised, too, by how much I missed you. I couldn't survive New Year's Eve without you. Can I stay with you or shall I go find a hotel?"

"Well, actually a hotel would be better. Come with me. I'll book you a room in an excellent one. You can leave your luggage here at the reception. Umberto, you'll take care of them, won't you?"

"Of course, Dottoressa! Don't worry about it!"

"Greg, come on, follow me!"

As soon as they got on the elevator, Greg tried to kiss Lory. She managed to avoid it and as she began to talk about the evening, she invited Greg to go to the ball with her. Once they arrived at Lory's flat, she offered him a seat and poured them each a cup of coffee. Suddenly, the day seemed to be getting long. She phoned the Savoy and booked a room for Greg.

"Now I have to go," she said. "I have an appointment with my hairdresser. And you need to go check in. The Savoy is close and it's an excellent hotel. You will like it! Fellini shot a film there. I'll call you a taxi."

"Thank you for being so nice to me. I'm sorry to have popped into your life so unexpectedly. But I am also happy to see you again and to be able to spend New Year's Eve with you!"

"OK, no problem. Your taxi will be here in five minutes, its number is Dondolo 116, so let's get you to the reception area to wait there. I'll walk you to the elevator."

They walked side by side in silence until they reached the elevator, which arrived almost immediately. Then Greg entered and turning toward Lory said, "Lory, I will commit suicide." The doors closed.

"What? Wait a minute! What are you saying?" cried Lory, but the elevator was already descending. She started to run downstairs, but when she reached the reception area, only Umberto was there. She opened the main door, went outside and looked around, but saw only the usual traffic. Her eyes filled with tears and she almost had a panic attack. She turned her face away from Umberto and hurried back to her flat. She decided to skip the hairdresser and followed Greg to the Savoy, almost paralyzed with fear. Self-accusation, love, sorrow, helplessness and anger for Greg's behavior all flashed through her mind. She became convinced that something must have happened to Greg since the last time she had seen him. He had been so very alive when she knew him. Now he seemed obsessed to be near her, which made her want to keep her distance, for which she felt guilty.

Lory called a taxi, put on her favorite tweed jacket, which could dress up anything, even her jeans, and went directly to the upscale Savoy. There, she asked the receptionist for Gregory Bellmont. Greg answered the call from reception immediately. The receptionist asked if he wanted to talk to Lory and gave her the receiver.

"Hi Lory! It's so nice that you are here! Come up! My room number is 512."

"All right, then, I'm coming up," Lory said breathing a sigh of relief having found Greg alive and kicking. While standing in the elevator she thought about telling him off for his awful behavior, frightening her with suicide and forcing and her to follow him to the hotel. But, by the time she reached Greg's room, she decided to speak to him carefully to keep his mood positive and to prevent him from doing harm to himself.

Greg opened the door with a bright smile. He took Lory into his arms, pulling her close to him, and kissed her passionately.

"I'm so happy that you are here!" he whispered into Lory's ear.

"Well, yes. You know..." Lory began to say that they needed to have a serious talk, but at the last minute decided not to spoil his happiness, which seemed to depended on her.

"Don't say anything!" Greg interrupted her. "Stay here with me at the hotel. Don't go home before the ball. We will buy you an incredible evening dress in the hotel boutique and go to the ball together. If you'd like, we can get you in with the hotel hairdresser. What do you think?"

"Excellent. Let's do that" Lory answered, resigning herself to forced happiness.

They managed to prepare for the ball. Lory went to the hotel hairdresser and Greg bought her a very expensive, beautiful scuba evening dress with a scarf made of shimmering blue silk. They were sitting in the taxi when Lory's mobile phone rang.

"Hello!" She answered.

"Hi Lory! It's Nick. Where are you? I couldn't reach you at home. I thought we could go to Veltmann's ball together."

"Oh, that would have been lovely, but I just can't, due to something unexpected that's come up. I'm really sorry! I'll explain everything at the Veltmanns'. We are on the way and will be there soon. Bye!"

"All right, as you wish. See you there! Bye-bye!"

Lory and Greg arrived at the Director's residence a few minutes later. Greg paid the taxi driver and they entered the crowded ball room gracefully. Lory's colleagues hardly recognized her in the luxurious dress, arm in arm with an unknown, very handsome and very elegant man.

"Dear Dottoressa Hennes, you are positively sparkling this evening! Will you introduce us your partner? I don't think we've met," Veltmann said, greeting them both.

"My dear, you look spectacular!" added Mrs. Veltmann while her husband and gave Lory a formal hug and a kiss on the face.

"This is is my friend, Gregory Bellmont."

"My Lady and Sir, it's nice to meet you and thank you for your hospitality and the opportunity to say farewell the old year and welcome the new year with you!" Greg responded politely to the host and his wife.

"It's our pleasure to have you with us, making our Dottoressa most charming she has been ever since we've known her!"

Lory tried to slip quietly into the crowd, which was not an easy task considering their spectacular appearance. Then the situation heated up, when Nick, unsuspecting, arrived alone.

Following a formal greeting with the Veltmanns, Nick immediately noticed Lory and headed towards her, when Greg appeared with two glasses of champagne in his hands. Nick recoiled at the sight of the tall, elegant, and very attractive man, but forced himself to say, "Dottoressa you are really beautiful this evening!" in a very formal manner. "Please, introduce me to your companion."

"Oh Nickolas, this is Mr. Gregory Bellmont, a very good, old friend of mine. Greg, please meet Mr. Nickolas de Bakker, Doctor of History, the Scientific Secretary of our Institute, and last but not least my new friend."

"Nice to meet you! To be honest, I don't know any of Lorain's family and friends," Nick responded.

"The pleasure is mutual! It is really comforting to know that Lorain already has good friends here, so far from home." The two men shook hands.

For the occasion, the Veltmanns opened the wall between the living room and dining room, creating one huge ball room with buffet tables around the perimeter. Chairs had been set up for the guests to rest between dances. Since the buffet had just opened, Lory invited her two suitors to select some of the beautifully arranged food. The chef outdid himself, again. He served a variety of small bites with salmon, Parma ham, truffles etc., and slices of cakes were lined up on silver trays. Lory and her companions, plates in hand, went to the other end of the room and found chairs near the Christmas tree. With Lory between them, the two men started to eat and talk. After some polite words, the conversation stopped and they ate in silence. Phil and Anna arrived, joining the group, greeting Lory and Nick first. Then they noticed Greg, whom Lory introduced politely. They sat down next to Nick and started into their food. The awkward silence was interrupted by Nick, who asked Lory if he could bring something to drink. She accepted and asked for a glass of punch. Then Phil took a seat near Greg and began to interrogate him.

"So, what do you do?"

"Currently, I live in Tokyo. My parents are on a diplomatic mission there and I'm attending a PhD program in economics at the University of Tokyo."

"That's fantastic! And may I ask how long you've known Lory?" Phil had stopped using the formal term Dotoressa, because he was proud to show his friendship with Lory.

"Of course. We met years ago on a summer holiday in Florida. We began talking on the flight there and were surprised to find that that we studied at the same university but in different departments."

"That's amazing!" Anna exclaimed.

"Our mutual, undeniable attraction was born suddenly during that first flight and lasts even today. Am I right, my dear?" Greg addressed his question to Lory just as Nick arrived with the drinks.

"Well, yes," Lory said trying to hide her embarrassment from the others. She thanked Nick for the punch and tasted it quickly. At the same moment, "Dream a Little Dream of Me" by Kahn/Andree/Schwandt began to play. Greg tossed his head and looked at Lory.

"Do you hear it, Lory? It's our song! Shall we dance?"

"Of course," Lory responded, putting her hand into Greg's, but gazing at Nick, who clearly looked disappointed and upset.

The dance floor was crowded, but during the dance, Lory kept trying to catch Nick's eye. Nick tried to avoid their sight and drank more and more punch. Lory intended to speak to Nick immediately after her dance with Greg, but Greg managed an upset, taking Lory by hand and leading her out to the terrace. There they sat down on wall and Greg told her how his life was hopeless and that he had no inclination to go back to Tokyo. He admitted that his only reason for living was Lory. She tried to affirm other reasons for living, like the importance of obtaining his PhD, but Greg continued his lamentation. He blamed his father for forcing him into PhD studies and said that he would go mad trying to live up to his father's expectations. He stated that one could learn everything they needed for a successful life in secondary school and beyond that all studies were useless. Of course, Lory disagreed, since her university studies made her the scientist she was. Finally, she gave up and accepted Greg's point of view, especially since he was kind enough to go inside and bring her scarf to cover her shoulders against the cold. He seemed willing to do anything, just to stay alone with her on the terrace. Eventually, he got up the courage to explain to her why he had let their relationship fade before he left for Japan three years before. Since then, they had exchanged letters only every few months and when Lory got the job in Rome, their contact had ended.

"Oh Lory! If you knew how much I suffered for letting you go. Then I visited your mother and she told me you had been in Rome for half a year. I decided to see you and explain it all to you and repair everything."

"But Greg...in reality there wasn't anything anymore between us. What is there to repair?"

"That's the point I'm trying to make, Lory! I want a relationship with you. A serious relationship. I want to make a family with you and only you!" Lory was genuinely surprised and didn't know what to say. She whispered, "This is all very nice Greg, but you know, in a real relationship, plans are made together. The desire to start a family together must also exist in my heart."

"Don't you love me? When we spent so much time together, going to the cinema, going to dinner...I felt your love."

"Everything was different in Amsterdam. But three years have passed and during all that time we have only corresponded, and not all that frequently. Don't misunderstand me, you are a wonderful guy, Greg, but I'm confused. You know what? Let's go back to the ball room and give this conversation a rest for the night. Let's sleep on it."

"All right. But tomorrow we can come back to it, can't we?"

"Yes, of course."

They returned to the ball room, where the atmosphere was festive. The New Year's Eve horns sounded loudly and confetti was falling everywhere. The contents of the buffet had changed to mini cakes and a wide range of sweets. Greg grabbed Lory's hand and pulled her toward the buffet. She was looking around to find Nick, but without no success. Fortunately, Phil and Anna were standing at the buffet table. Lory asked them if they knew where Nick was. Phil's answer surprised her.

"He said he needed some fresh air, and having an invitation to a ball at the Spanish Institute on the San Pietro in Montorio, he went there. I called him a taxi because he was totally drunk."

"What a pity! Do you think he plans to come back?"

"To be honest, I don't have the faintest idea what's making him so very sad, but it'll be a miracle if he can make it home tonight, being as drunk as he is."

"Why do you think he got drunk out of sorrow?"

"In the last few years, I've attended a lot of receptions, parties and balls with Nick, but he has never got drunken. This is the first time. And the vacant look he had while he was here… something big trouble must be troubling him. Can I ask you a personal question? Is it possible that he's fallen in love with you and is jealous of Greg?"

"Why would you think of that, Sherlock?"

"Only because we've spent a lot of time together in the Institute and gotten to know each other. When I asked him, he answered me honestly, being drunk, and asked nervously if you and Greg were still outside on the terrace."

"Yes, but he could have left out of loneliness or boredom."

"Bored and lonely in his beloved Institute where he is in close friendship with every colleague? He feels at home here. Don't be ridiculous, Lory! I feel bad for him, imagining him going outcast to spend New Year's Eve among young scholars at the Cervantes Institute."

"Do you have an invitation to the Spanish Institute ball, by any chance?"

"No, I'm sorry I don't. I don't think anyone in our institute has, except for Nick. He is the only one here who keeps an active relationship with the Cervantes Institute."

"That's too bad! I must find a way to talk to him."

"You are too late for this year."

"That's impossible!"

"What is impossible, my dear?" Greg arrived at that exact moment.

"My dear…" Phil mimicked, "you won't reach to him this year." Then he took Anna's hand and headed toward the sweets.

Lory stood, paralyzed, unable to hear or focus, as she started to understand what a big mistake she had made. She should have gone to talk with Nick, rather than going out to the terrace with Greg. Eventually, she realized that Greg was calling to invite her to have some cake.

"What's with you, my dear?" Greg asked, louder.

"Please, don't call me my dear! It makes me uncomfortable. We aren't really together."

"I wanted to do this tomorrow, but it seems this is the right moment. So, I need to tell you that I can't live without you. I think of nothing but you. Will you marry me?"

The music had stopped and Greg's question sounded sharply across the ball room, making everybody look up suddenly.

"What?" Lory asked, deeply surprised.

"Miss Lorain Hennes, will you marry me?" Greg repeated in front of everyone present in the room. His voice was low, but very but firm.

Lory struggle with the love she felt for each of the two men. How could she make a choice between the growing love and mutual desire she had with Nick and the pain of her dear, old friend, and former love, Greg, who was considering suicide without her. She felt Greg did not deserve to be let down by the sweetest manifestation of love he ever felt in his life. With the crowd staring at her, she had to make her choice immediately. So, she decided.

"Yes. I will marry you," said, meeting the crowd's expectation.

Loud cheers erupted in the ball room, the Veltmanns being the first to congratulate the newly betrothed couple. The Director spoke to the crowd.

"Dear Guests, my friends, as the Director of this Institute it is my duty and pleasure to announce the official engagement of our Dottoressa Lorain Hennes to this enchanting young man, Mr. Gregory Bellmont! Three cheers for the new couple!"

"Hip, hip, hurray! Hip, hip, hurray! Hip, hip, hurray!" The room echoed with the cries as guests lifted glasses of champagne, which the waiters had quickly filled.

Lory, overwhelmed by her emotions, turned to leave the room, one step at a time. It was nearly midnight so everybody was occupied with the arrival of the New Year. None of them noticed Lory's leaving except for Greg, who followed her.

"Where are you going, my dear? It's time to welcome the New Year. Come on, let's clink!" he said holding his glass toward Lory.

"We can drink to the New Year here, outside, alone. I'm tired of being in a crowd."

"What a great idea! It's much more romantic! I'll tell you when it's time to drink to our future. It's a few minutes to midnight." He sat down beside Lory on one of the stone walls of the terrace. From inside they could hear the crowd yelling, "Happy New Year," so they drank. Then Greg gave Lory a light kiss on the lips.

"I am so happy, Lory! Can I stay with you tonight?" he asked his future bride.

"Yes, of course. It would be silly to go back to the hotel, although I would prefer if you did."

"Don't you want to spend our engagement night together, sleeping in my arms?"

"I do, but I'm so tired," Lory said weakly, thinking she was not built for the perfect, passionate love she imagined with Nick, which both excited and frightened her, being unpredictable and unknown. She made her choice out of a sense of duty to her old friend, who was falling to pieces without her. She mused that she could return Greg's love. After all, she had loved him before. Greg needed to be saved and she would sacrifice her desire to experience the mutual desire she felt for Nick. She thought about all love stories she had read about heroic knights. It made it easier to accept the difficult decision she had made in Greg's favor. Handsome, strong, chivalrous Greg was so like a noble knight or a prince. Lory decided to be satisfied and even happy with the idea of a predictable marriage and the safe future that Greg wanted and could give her. A kind of euphoric happiness swept over her as she replayed the fairy tale that seemed to have come true for her earlier that evening. The situation made her feel special and chosen. After sitting in silence side by side, Greg took her hand and pulled her up.

"You are tired my dear. I'll take you home," he said.

Lory nodded and followed him obediently. The night was calm and pleasant. They spent the whole night sleeping, chastely, in each other's arms.

CHAPTER SEVEN

New Year – New Life

The next morning, they woke up in each other's arms, as they had fallen asleep. After the previous busy day, Lory was happy to stay in bed longer than the usual, so she got up a bit before eight o'clock. Leaving the bed, she realized that her future spouse was also awake.

"Everything that happened to us yesterday seems incredible" Lory said to the still sleepy Greg.

"Good morning, my dear! How did you sleep?" he replied.

"Well, thank you. Imagine! I had a dream of our wedding."

"You know what? Let's have breakfast at the Savoy! What do you think?"

"I say yes! You sure know how to live! I'll go get ready. Then after breakfast you can check out of the hotel and come to stay with me."

"Okay. But I do understand if you don't want to share your flat with me before our marriage. I mean if it is awkward for you because of your colleagues, I can stay at the hotel."

"Don't worry! We don't live in the middle ages and we got officially engaged in front of them. I just can't believe it!"

"Are you happy?"

"Yes! And you?"

"Me too, very much!"

"But there is one thing to do. I have to speak to Nick before we go to the Savoy."

"He may still be sleeping, don't you think? What can be so important? Your colleagues told me he had gone to another party last night, so he must have returned home very late."

"I know, but I need to talk with him as soon as possible."

"All right. I'll wait for you here."

"Thanks! I'll be back soon!" she said going to wash her face and put on a nice Audrey Hepburn style dress as quickly as she could.

She didn't phone to Nick, intentionally. She supposed he would be hurt and might not be willing to talk with her. Instead, she took the risk that he might slam the door in her face. When she got to his flat, she stopped short holding her finger over the buzzer and waited a moment, taking a deep breath before ringing the bell. After a few minutes she heard Nick's voice.

"Just a minute. I'm coming!" His shuffling steps sounded from inside.

Then the door opened and the tousled and unshaven Nick was standing in front of her, wearing only boxer shorts and a tee shirt.

"Hi Nick. Good morning. I have to talk to you."

"Hi. What are you doing here? What have we got to talk about? I guess I should congratulate you. I hear you got engaged to Greg yesterday."

"Yes, but it's not that simple! With you we have..."

"Well, it seems simple to me," Nick interrupted her. "Don't worry, Lory. I got there too, late, that's all. There is nothing to apologize for, nothing really happened between us."

"But something wonderful might have happened, and I..."

"We'll never know, will we?" he interrupted her again. "So, just enjoy your happiness. How long will Greg be staying here? When do you intend to hold the wedding?"

"We haven't decided. But I'll let you know you, for sure."

"All right, thank you. That's very nice of you. Our friendship deserves at least that much, doesn't it?"

"Of course! So, we're to remain friends?" Lory asked searching Nick's face, hoping. When he nodded she responded, "You have no idea how happy you've made me!"

"Now go and enjoy your engagement!"

"Thank you, Nick!" she kissed his face and turning on her heel, returned to her flat.

Greg was waiting for her, ready to leave for the hotel.

"How did things go with that little runt?" he asked.

"Don't talk about him that way. It couldn't have gone better. And just because he's slim, he doesn't deserve your mockery!"

"OK. I'm sorry!"

"It's OK. Let's go in my car." Lory led the way.

The atmosphere at the Savoy as always was grand, respectful and elevating.

"It's amazing that time stopped centuries ago in these luxury hotels. They make you feel like you rule the world," Lory stated entering the hall of the Savoy.

"Yes, my dear, you will have to get accustomed to it, because I plan to take you only to places like this. You deserve the best and more!"

Flattered, Lory accepted Greg's words with pleasure, knowing that he was likely exaggerating. It was past breakfast time at the hotel, so they went to the cafeteria. While they ate, they talked about their future and their plans, focusing on their immediate next steps. They agreed that Greg would return to Tokyo next Saturday to share the news with his parents and complete his PhD. In the meantime, Lory would share their plans with her parents. They also decided to keep in contact daily by Skype, until the Easter holidays, when they would meet again in Rome or Tokyo. In the meanwhile, Lory promised to take her fiancé to the most romantic, historic and artistic sites in Rome and its surroundings, like Villa Adriana, Villa d'Este in Tivoli, the ruins of the villa and city of Nero in Anzio, the small Etruscan cities like Cerveteri, Sutri, Capranica and other beautiful medieval small towns like Palestrina, Fumone and, last but not least, the Montecassino Abbey.

"There are an infinite number of historical sites to see, but we have only three days, since your flight departs Saturday at dawn," Lory stated.

"We can leave some site for the Easter holidays or later, when I join you here, after defending my PhD. I'll move in with you and find a a job in Rome."

"This is so...fantastic!" Lory stuttered, with deep emotion. "You tell me this great news just like that! In the next few months, I will start working with our contacts at the Institute to find job offers that suit your talents."

"That would be excellent. I will do my best. I promise! Now that we've made plans, let's go check out of the hotel before they make me pay for an extra day."

They went upstairs to Greg's room and packed his bags. There wasn't much to repack, since Greg barely occupied his room and spent almost no time there. After they finished packing they had time for a romantic kiss before heading to reception with the key. They got into Loy's car just before ten o'clock.

The city was calm and quite deserted, so they reached the Institute in just a few minutes. Then they unpacked Greg's bags and Lory made a pasta al tonno for lunch.

"This is so tasty. I've never eaten a dish like this! How'd you become such a good cook?" Greg praised her cooking extravagantly.

"Come on! You must be kidding. This is the easiest and quickest dish to make in the world. In the Netherlands, kids are going crazy for this. Even my mom learned the recipe and had great success with it."

"I believe it, because it is celestial. It tastes a bit hot but the tuna and tomatoes compensate nicely. I don't really know much about Italian food, except for the pizzas and pastas that are available everywhere."

"Those aren't as good as what they make here with original Italian ingredients. Since I know how much you like to eat, prepare yourself for a gourmet tour, too! While we explore Rome, we will also try the very best, meaning the most typically Italian, restaurants," Lory smiled planning their upcoming tour.

"All right. Since today's January first, I assume most places are closed. Let's stay home today, and take a bottle of champagne and a couple of glasses to the bedroom." Greg opened the fridge, took out a bottle of champagne, and scooping Lory up, headed to the bedroom. "We can return for the glasses later" he added, placing her on the bed...

It was late when they woke up from their passionate love making. They put on their robes, and with champagne glasses in hand went out on the terrace. The weather was mild and lovely, in spite of it being winter.

"This winter is more pleasant than usual in Rome," Lory stated.

"Maybe that's just the heat of our love," Greg winked.

"Yes, of course, my dear!"

The following days passed as planned. Since Veltmann gave Lory time off, she took Greg to the the famous sites in Rome and nearby, and they ate in typical Italian restaurants. Their three days together passed very quickly. Early Saturday morning, Lory took Greg to the airport and waited with him until he check in. Then after saying good-bye and giving each other a kiss, they promised they would speak every day and went their own ways.

CHAPTER EIGHT

Long Distance Relationship

Lory's spirits were still flying with the euphory of her engagement, when her mother's phone call brought her back down to Earth.

"But, my dear," her mother said, "are you sure about this? Don't misunderstand, me. Your father and I want just you to be happy. Will this choice really make you happy?"

"Yes mom, it really will make me happy. What can I do to persuade you to accept it?"

"We do accept it, my dear. Our only concern is how quickly it all happened. You have all the time you want to make such a serious decision."

"Mom, I'm twenty-eight. I graduated three years ago and got my PhD last year. And, if you haven't noticed, I'm also holding down a great job. Perhaps I'm old enough and prepared enough to decide when to take such an important step in my life. It's simply the right time."

"All right, if you're convinced. We are happy with your decision to establish your own family with a great guy like Greg. So, have you decided any of the wedding details? When and where do you want to hold it? I hope here, in the Netherlands?"

"We haven' fixed a date or place yet, but we have decided that Greg will move in with me in Rome after he's gotten his PhD. In the meantime, we will talk to each other every day and we will spend our Easter holiday together."

"Sounds like you've made some good plans. I'm so happy!"

"I'm grateful for your support and understanding!"

"Of course, my dear!"

"I've got to go now, mom. Lots of hugs and kisses to you and dad. Good-bye."

"Bye-bye, my dear!"

Telling her parents about the engagement took a weight off Lory's mind and legitimized it at the same time. She was looking forward to hearing how Greg's parents reacted to hearing about their plans. As agreed, Greg called her at dawn on Sunday, which was almost noon in Tokyo. He reported he had arrived without incident and promised to share the big news with his parents and Skype Lory immediately after. His conversation with his parents went well, so while Skyping in the middle of the night in Rome, they decided to hold the wedding in Amsterdam. Since Greg's parents weren't religious, they decided to hold a civil ceremony. They agreed that Lory should begin planning and that they would sign the required paperwork in Amsterdam over the Easter holidays.

Their first challenge was the eight hour time difference between Tokyo and Rome. Lory stayed up until midnight every day so that Greg could call her at eight a.m. Tokyo time. After some exhausting experiments trying to find the right time to talk, it became routine. The regularity of their Skype dates increased their sense of security in the decision they had made and reassured them both. Time passed quickly, and soon it was spring. Over the past few months their parents had also gotten accustomed to their relationship.

Meanwhile, Lory threw herself into the rewarding work of planning the next exhibition to follow the Van Gogh exhibit. It was scheduled to opening right before Easter. She felt she had to outdo her previous success. After weighing her options, she decided to focus on a classic Dutch painter, Jan Vermeer van Delft, the creator of the "The Northern Mona Lisa." Vermeer van Delft had been unknown for centuries, recognized only by his contemporaries, although, in modern times he was considered the second greatest painter of the golden age of Dutch painters, after Rembrandt. Lory put the idea to Veltmann, who agreed to fully support the exhibit.

After uninstalling the Van Goghs, she began contacting permanent collections and museums in possession of Vermeer van Delft works. As a result of the robbery, she paid even more attention to every detail, every step of the process, for the new exhibit and insisted that her colleagues do the same. The arrangements proceeded well and the opening ceremony was scheduled for March 21st, a week before Holy Thursday, the celebration of Christ's last supper. Lory intended to travel home to Maastricht that weekend, the beautiful Catholic town where she was raised. While Lory's parents supported plans for a civil wedding in Greg's home town of Amsterdam, Lory, as a Catholic, would have preferred a religious ceremony, declaring their oath of love before God. But her parents' support for a civil ceremony reassured her of the sacred legitimacy of making a such a covenant in public, even if not in a church. Greg's mother put in for the marriage license. The license would only be valid after Lory and Greg signed it, which they planned to do on the Monday of Holy Week, once they had both arrived in Amsterdam. Until then, they could not set a wedding date.

For Lory, the opening ceremony of the Vermeer van Delft exhibition was like the last step of a 110 meter hurdle race, especially since she was leaving for the the Netherlands the next day. She made sure all of her colleagues, including Mark Poten, the new accountant, fully understood all of the tasks and authorizations assigned to them. After having arranged everything and planned all contingencies, she packed her bags Friday evening and Skyped Greg one last time before meeting him in Amsterdam.

"My dear, I've been looking forward this moment. It seemed Easter would never arrive. My PhD program is so boring. But it makes my dad happy and I'm only doing it for him."

"Don't be silly. Your father wants the best for you and you will need that PhD to find the job you want in Rome," Lory responded, as usual, trying to keep him focused on their future together. "Time has been flying here because you are my goal and to achieve it, I had to accelerate my work schedule to get everything organized so I can leave the office for a while to meet you in Amsterdam."

"My future wife is such a clever bunny! I'm so proud to be marrying a girl like you. We should hang up, now. I don't want you to miss your flight tomorrow morning. Kisses! I can't wait to see you in Amsterdam! Good-bye."

"Bye-bye and good night, my dear. Have a pleasant flight. Kisses to you, too!"

The trip went well. Nick insisted on taking Lory to the airport and waited with her until she checked in. The flight was smooth and she arrived to Amsterdam in an hour and a half. Her parents were waiting for her. According to plan, they stayed with Greg's parents, Dave and Gabrielle (Gabi) Bellmont, who had a large flat and had left Tokyo earlier, before Greg was to return home for the holidays. Staying in the flat together provided an excellent opportunity to get know each other. It also made preparing for the wedding easier. They all enjoyed their time together. mutual respect and kindness the parents showed each other seemed to be the start of a great friendship, too. Greg arrived in Amsterdam Sunday evening. Lory and his parents met him at the airport.

Things went well, starting with a great family dinner Sunday evening and continuing Monday morning, when Greg and Lory completed the marriage application at the registry office. They arranged the particulars of the ceremony with the registrar, selecting July 27th, a Saturday, for the wedding. They hoped that with so much notice, their guests would be able to take the day off. By noon, they finished at the registry and the couple went to buy wedding rings. Greg, embarrassed to have proposed to Lory without an engagement ring, looked forward to making up for his deficiency. After considering a variety of wedding ring options, they chose minimalist, unpolished golden wedding rings with an ornate wavy etching. Lory's brother, Steve, bought the rings while Greg paid for Lory's engagement ring. Steve had known Greg for a long time and supported the marriage. Steve was the pianist in a rock band on tour in Europe, but planned to be back in time for the wedding. Greg's sister, Angelique she was living in Sweden with her husband Matts and their daughter Sonja. She held two challenging jobs teaching Spanish language at a both a state and a private secondary school in Malmö. Therefore, she couldn't join the family until the wedding.

The Easter Holidays passed very quickly. On the April 2nd Lory returned to Rome, her parents to Maastricht, and Greg and his parents to Tokyo. They were all pleased with the wedding plans they had arranged. They had divided the costs and tasks among themselves to ensure the ceremony and the following party would be perfect. During the holiday they had put together a list of 150 guests and Lory's parents took responsibility for mailing the invitations that Lory and Greg had selected.

Nick was waiting for Lory in Rome at Fiumicino Airport, drove her home and invited her for lunch. They talked about the Easter holidays and the wedding preparations. Nick updated Lory on happenings at the Institute and accompanied her to the gallery to reassure her that everything was fine. After they returned to Nick's flat, Lory admitted she was tired and needed some rest. She thanked Nick for the lunch and for his kindness and went to her flat to take a shower, empty her suitcase, and nap for a while. That evening she couldn't speak with Greg, since he and his parents were flying over Asia, which made her feel a little uneasy. She was eager to hear from her fiancé. The emotional bond growing between them surprised her. It seemed like a celestial attraction was binding them together which amused and calmed her at the same time. While in Amsterdam, they had developed their own "love island". When they were together, the world ceased to exist around them.

Wednesday evening, when Greg called Lory to inform her of their arrival, the couple quickly returned to their own special relationship with their unique love language. The long distance relationship became routine again and they managed it well.

Work at the Institute proceeded well, too, as Lory slid back into both her routines and new tasks. Her relationship with Nick was smooth and their friendship made Lory happy. In the meantime, Anna receive a one-year scholarship to Barcelona. She would start next September, but promised Lory she would be to be present at her wedding.

In June, Greg defended his PhD and began to pack his bags. He and Lory decided to send his belongings to Amsterdam, where he could select which items to take to Rome. As they neared their wedding day, the Greg became more and more anxious. Their big day became the central topic of their conversations.

"You know, my dear, I really don't like being the center of attention and being stared at by a crowd. I'm only doing this for you."

"Don't worry, my dear. It's normal to feel anxious. It will pass. In front of the registrar, we'll be back on our own love island and the crowd of guests will disappear. You'll see, everything will be all right!"

"I hope so."

Greg moved back to Amsterdam at the end of June, followed by his parents, who completed their diplomatic duties a week later. Lory's parents were staying in Amsterdam at Greg's family flat and Lory joined them Sunday morning June 30th. Lory had decided to wear her mother's wedding dress, which she left with the dressmaker for alteration during the Easter holidays. When she went to try it on, it fit perfectly, so, she brought it back to the flat. The excitement began to grow with the arrival of the guests, who stopped by to personally deliver their gifts to the bride and the groom. The flat was soon full of people and presents, so Lory took charge of the gift opening ceremony herself. Her biggest surprise was that several of her colleagues from the Institute had come to attend the wedding as well, except for Nick, who didn't particularly care to watch her marry another man, Mark Poten, Gigi, Umberto and Antonio who were taking care of the Institute. Everything felt perfect as the big day finally arrived.

CHAPTER NINE

The Wedding

The day of the wedding everybody was very busy preparing the bride, while Greg and his parents received the guests at the Registry before the ten o'clock start of the ceremony. Everyone had been invited to the party afterwards, organized in the Ciel Blue hall on the 23rd floor of the luxurious Hotel Okura. The hotel was situated along one of the most beautiful canals in the most prominent district of Amsterdam, about a fifteen minute drive from the Schiphol Airport, so guests could reach it easily.

Finally, the bride arrived at the Registry wearing a marvelous sleeveless, minimalist style, white satin dress. The only ornament was its train. By then, the crowd of the guests had taken their seats in the hall and Greg was standing in front of the Registrar, waiting for his bride. Lory walked down the aisle on her father's arm to "Dream a Little Dream of Me" followed by Mendelsohn's Wedding March. After that the Registrar gave a long, heartwarming speech and the couple said their oaths and "I dos." Then Greg kissed Lory, his lips barely touching hers. The bride and groom signed the marriage certificate and related documents, witnessed by Lory's best friend, Juliette Sella, and Greg's best friend, Joseph Majer. Afterwards the newly married couple and their parents received greetings and good wishes from the guests and everyone departed for the Hotel Okura. There, the best man, Anthony Nice, Lory's father's best friend, was waiting for them and invited everybody to join in a toast. The orchestra was playing discretely in the background, creating a lovely atmosphere. It was just after noon by the time all the guest arrived and took their seat at the ornately decorated tables. The best man formally greeted the guests and Lory's and Greg's fathers each gave speeches. After that, an extraordinary dinner was served. Between the courses the young couple separated temporarily to greet the guests personally at their seats. They returned to the table just in time for the arrival of the wedding cake, cut it, and gave a slice to each guest. Then it was time to dance, starting with a first waltz led by the newlyweds. But Greg had disappeared, so Lory and her father had to start the dance. Soon afterwards everyone dropped their formalities, talking, eating, dancing and drinking freely throughout the hall.

Lory began to wonder if Greg was avoiding her. She was very hurt that Greg hadn't danced with her. She had looked forward to photos of them dancing together, in her wedding dress. However, her desire went unsatisfied all evening. The best man and the parents remain until the end of the party to say farewell to every guest, so Lory and Greg could retire for their wedding night to a room booked for them in the hotel. Greg took Lory in his arms and picked her up, carrying her over the doorstep for their first night of married life together. But as soon he set her down on the bed, he asked her if she minded not making love, since they had done it before and already knew each other intimately. He added that a love as sublime as theirs could overcome every profane desire. What could Lory say? She accepted her husband's decision, but felt deeply hurt. She decided to let it go, hoping it was just a fluke and trusting that their love was true and passionate and they would have a wonderful future together.

CHAPTER TEN

Initial Difficulties

The morning after the wedding night, they slept in longer than usual and decided to check out the hotel swimming pool. Greg, wanting some company, invited his witness, Joseph, Joseph's wife, Andrea, and Lory's witness, Julie, to join them. They all accepted the invitation happily and reached the wedding suite in a few minutes where they change into bathing suits and headed to the pool together, joking and laughing. Lory's favorite moment was when Julie noticed some rice still sticking to her hair which had puffed up in the water. While swimming and sunbathing, Joseph and Andrea announced the impending arrival of their second baby and invited the new couple to play cards with them in the evenings, before going back to Rome.

After a while, the friends said good-bye and the newlyweds returned to their wedding suite, got dressed and left the hotel. Arriving at Greg's parents' flat they found Greg's sister and her family and Lory's parents. They cheered the arrival of the new couple and asked if they were satisfied with the ceremony and party. Lory was eager for some peaceful time alone with her husband, but Greg had arranged a variety of activities for them, playing cards, swimming, going to concerts, the cinema, the theatre, museums, exhibitions, lunches, dinners, and so on, always accompanied by friends. Outside of these activities, he left Lory alone for hours, visiting his gay friend, Leslie Talbot. This active social life continued all the summer. Then it was the time to return to Rome.

"Finally," Lory thought, "he won't be able to avoid spending some time alone with me!" Lory couldn't wait to be alone with her husband.

They arrived in Rome at the end of August. Antonio was waiting for them at Fiumicino Airport, receiving them with congratulations for their marriage. They had so much luggage that it barely fit into the Audi, the Institute's official car. On the ride back to their apartment, Lory interrogated Antonio on all the happenings at the Institute during the summer, while at the same time pointing out Roman monuments to Greg. Greg was very interested in history, arts and literature, which was one of the reasons Lory was convinced they were made for each other. This time, instead of exploring the Eternal City, they had to find Greg a job while Lory got reaccustomed to the rhythm of her work. But on the weekends, they went walking in the historical center or on touristy excursions to the countryside.

It turned out that finding a job was fairly easy for Greg. He spoke Italian well, having completed an Italian language course at the Italian Cultural Institute in Tokyo. He had also earned a scholarship and spent a month studying Italian in Perugia, a few years ago. He kept up with his Italian practice and was now fluent. Consequently, by the end of September, they found him a job, with some help from Veltmann, who informed Greg of a vacancy at John Cabot University. It seemed like a terrific opportunity, so Greg applied right away. He was called for a job interview the same week and told to be ready to start work the following Monday. Lory, to celebrate, organized a romantic dinner for two at home by candle light. It had a magical effect on Greg, who finally made a passionate love with his wife. Lory was in heaven and was sure that their romantic life together would improve from then on.

Greg started his new job on Monday, September 30th. It was a particularly lovely day. That evening, Lory planned another romantic candle lit dinner at home to celebrate Greg's new job and get his first impressions. The dinner was great and they talked about Greg's work, but the evening did not end the way Lory had expected. Greg retired right after dinner, telling Lory he was tired. Lory had to accept what Greg had stated several times – physical intimacy was not a priority for him in their marriage.

Once the academic year began, Greg became very busy. Their private life fell into a daily routine. Still, they made time for lovely week-ends together, going for walks in the city center, visiting exhibits and museums, and going on excursions in the countryside. In addition, Greg decided to take windsurfing lessons starting in the spring. Lory interpreted Greg's latest amusements as replacements for the lack of the joy in their intimate life. Her feeling was strengthened by Greg's latest hobby, cooking. He spent a lot of time reading recipes and looking for special ingredients. As a result, they went frequently to the fish market in Fiumicino, to the famous Castroni groceries and markets in Rome, and even to collect marrons, a species of Australian crayfish, in the Castelli Romani, to buy strawberries in Nemi etc.

With Greg's new job, he also made new friends, mostly among his colleagues, so their social life became more active. He began hosting events at Lory's flat. Invitations were accepted and returned with pleasure. These new friendships grew and soon they were going to the theater, museums, exhibits, concerts, and the cinema with their new friends. In addition, one of Greg's first actions in Rome was to enroll them both at Sport Hotel Villa Pamphili, where each day they either swam early in the morning before work or worked out gym in the afternoon. All of this would have been fine, if Lory had felt desirable, like the healthy female half of a couple in love. But, to their friends, they seemed to be the luckiest couple and most of the women she knew envied her.

Every now and then, Greg mentioned being propositioned by homosexuals, especially at the gym, but he told Lory not to worry about it. He added that it was amusing, he'd gotten used to it, and he could handle it just fine. He told her long before their wedding that he had been sexually abused at the age of 10 by a gay man in a shower cabana at the beach, but he never shared any details. While Greg was politically liberal, he avoided voicing any opinion on the question of homosexuality in public. He liked to provoke those with more conservative views, pointing out their lack of open-mindedness and tolerance.

Later, that year, Lory was again hurt by his husband's behavior, when in the middle of November, he asked her go to Amsterdam alone to deal with some banking and administrative issues, using the airplane ticket provided her by the Ministry for the winter holidays. He intended to use his free ticket in December, planning to leave Lory alone in Rome for Christmas. Lory's mother objected, telling Greg, "If it is a problem for you, I will buy a ticket for Lory myself, but she will spend Christmas with us either way!"

"All right, mom. It's not a problem. We will pay for Lory's ticket, if it is so important," Greg stuttered.

"Of course, it is! What were you thinking?" she ended the discussion.

As the frequency of their travel, excursions, and adventures increased, their intimate life worsened. Greg did not show any physical desire toward Lory, even during the Christmas holidays. Lory became resentful and decided to speak to him.

"But we've already spoken about this and agreed that sexuality is not of primary importance in our marriage," Greg said.

"Right now, it couldn't be of any less importance!" Lory answered heatedly.

"Don't worry, it will be OK. Living in Japan, Japanese women just weren't attractive to me, so I went without a love affair for so long I became too accustomed to my own company. Don't worry and trust me." Greg's explanation calmed Lory down and she felt relieved.

After that, Lory figured she had license to use every trick she knew to seduce her husband, even though she felt it should have been his role to seduce her. She bought the sexiest lingerie she could find and put it on for Greg, but without result. He had no reaction, rejecting her rather impolitely. On the weekends she took him to the most romantic places she could think of, but also without results. Her husband never even held her hand or put an arm around her. She even organized a picnic at a picturesque beach rimmed with with marvelous rocks and junipers, but Greg sat two meters from where Lory had spread their plaid blanket, despite the fact that they were completely alone. Several months passed this way, Greg giving no sign that he noticed Lory's suffering. Just when she'd begin wondering if he still loved her, he'd make some strong and sincere statement of his intentions for their future together, and Lory convince herself that he just needed more time. For example, he made a point of saying that if they couldn't have their own baby, regardless of who's fault it was, they would stay together and adopt an orphan.

Greg had taken to using childish language, calling Lory his bunny and expecting her to call him her teddy bear. Once while they stood together at the Trevi Fontain, he said that he wished they were Smurfs living in the cave under the statue of Neptune, safe from the rest of the world, where he would fish to feed Lory and their children.

Lory began to think that her husband had psychological problems caused by some trauma and that he was trying to escape the real world. She had to admit that her husband had two faces, one for the public and another for his his wife. He showed his real face only to her, treating her at times like his mother and at others like a friend. At first, she thought that his ambiguity and weakness were due to his parents' divorce. His father now lived with his second wife, Gabi, and hadn't been able to provide emotional support to Greg after the divorce and the death of Greg's mother, a few years ago.

Lory also realized there was nothing she could do about his lack of attention to her needs. All her attempts were vain and the gap between them grew larger and larger. However, in public, they showed no sign of the increasing distance in their private life. Quite the contrary. Greg was caring and devoted to Lory when they were around others. They seemed to be the most devoted couple in the world.

They spent the upcoming Christmas holidays with Lory's parents and traveled around the Netherlands, visiting relatives and friends. For New Year's Eve they stayed at a friend's house. Their winter vacation passed quickly and soon they returned to Rome, back to their daily routine with all its problems. Meanwhile, Lory decided to take a different, less direct approach to reach Greg. She felt the best way to set Greg free from his emotional pain was to help talk about it. She did this in the hope that it might also liberate her husband from his physical inhibitions. To her happy surprise, the strategy worked, bringing them much closer to each other emotionally. Greg opened up to Lory and talked about his various painful experiences, like the sexual abuse he suffered while studying in Perugia, at the hands of an elderly man who started a conversation with him at the gym, feigning friendship, and invited him to his flat. According to Greg, it was only there that it became clear to him that the man was gay, when he played a homosexual hard porn film and tried to molest Greg. Greg didn't go into details, so Lory didn't know how far the man managed to get with him sexually. She became convinced that unpleasant experiences like these contributed to Greg's lack of masculinity and difficulty being physically intimate with her. Greg's painful past didn't shake her love for him, but her love became full of pity, which was less attractive than her previous view of him as a knight in shining armor. Lory did everything she could not to let her husband see the change in how she viewed him, since nobody wants to be loved out of pity. She tried to rekindle the fire of her previous love for Greg. Greg also did his best, trying to win his wife's affection with flowers and far more expensive presents.

Later, that winter, Greg's parents invited the couple to visit them in Japan. Veltmann agreed to give Lory leave for their voyage to Tokyo before Easter and the opening of the upcoming Rembrandt exhibit she had planned. Lory's heart was full of hope for a radical change in their relationship over the course of their long trip together.

CHAPTER ELEVEN

Japan

Greg's parents welcomed them, visibly happy to see them. Greg's father, Holland's ambassador to Tokyo, arranged for them to stay at the residence and suggested that Greg show his wife the place, having lived there for several years. Greg really liked the idea and Lory was happy to oblige.

While in Tokyo, Greg's parents showed them around the city so they could experience the pulsing life of the metropolis and some of its hidden parks and most famous restaurants together. Greg's father also provided an official car and driver so they could visit some of Japan's most beautiful sites.

Their first excursion out of Tokyo was to Kyoto, which deeply enchanted Lory. She always felt a special affection for the history, harmony and wisdom of the cultures of the Far East. Their excursion to the peak of Mount Fuji was like a miracle for her. They started with a walk along the base of the mountain in an immense magical forest, where the forest floor was covered with hydrangeas. Considering the time of year, the hydrangeas were only beginning to bud, but their tourist guide book contained pictures in full bloom, a fabulous sight. It was terribly cold at the top of the mountain so they quickly donned their coats. The view from the peak to the ocean and its shore was breathtaking. But the best part of the experience for Lory, beside the view, was the emotion she felt when Greg took her hand and whispered in her ear how happy he was to share his adventures and emotions with her. By the time they returned to the residence, they were exhausted by the long excursion. After dinner with

Greg's parents, they went to bed, gave each other a good-night kiss and fell asleep immediately.

Their next trip led them to Akita, then to Honjō and Nikoho, where they could learn more about the everyday lives of the Japanese. Lory had never eaten so much sushi before, and she had to admit it was not as bad as what she had tasted at the Japanese restaurant in Rome.

Their most exciting adventure was a shark hunting trip on bord a specially constructed and equipped yacht. Greg participated in the hunt with great enthusiasm, while Lory struggled with sea sickness brought on by the unpredictable fast acceleration and hard breaking of the yacht. Lory was eager to feel solid ground under her feet and still felt dizzy after their arrival home. Still, she was enchanted by the attention, thoughtfulness and availability of the Japanese on the yacht in response to her sea sickness. She also observed how seriously the Japanese took personal hygiene, a necessity due to the permanent high humidity of the Islands. She learned that, due to high humidity, the world famous Japanese gardens used special insecticides to care for the flowers and plants.

Their last activity in Japan was to serve as members of the jury at a beauty contest, with Greg's father, Dave. While judging, they had to sit on the ground on special mats, cross-legged. Lory didn't mind sitting sitting cross-legged with the Japanese members of the jury, but Dave and Greg suffered quite a bit that evening.

As they said farewell, Lory and Greg invited his parents to visit them in Rome during the summer holidays, which Dave and Gabi accepted happily.

CHAPTER TWELVE

Back in Rome

They arrived home in time for Lory to lead the uninstallation of the Rembrandt exhibition and prepare for the next one dedicated to Hieronymus Bosch. She selected the controversial painter because of the general theme of his paintings, which was whipping humans for their weaknesses and sins. In a way Lory was whipping herself, as well. She believed she was to blame for her problematic private life with Greg. She felt that she had sinned in her continual desire for the physical fulfilment of their love. It was only much later that she came to understand that desire is a normal part of a marriage. At the beginning of their marriage, Lory admired Greg for his ability to resist physical attraction and the desire for intimacy. She thought this in spite of the fact that her mother and friends all believed there was nothing more wonderful in the world than making love in the sacrament of marriage. She felt morally confused, which manifested in her choice of painter for the upcoming exhibit. Regardless of Lory's reasons for selecting the works of Bosh, the exhibit was a great success. The opening ceremony on March 23rd attracted more people than the Rembrandt exhibit.

The next Sunday was Palm Sunday. Lory had recently decided to return to the comfort of her former religious practice during the Easter holidays. She informed Greg of her intent to return to Roman Catholicism. Greg was very surprised and also irritated that they would be unable to go for excursions during the holidays, due to her commitment to attending masses. He never considered joining Lory for Catholic services at the Vatican. Instead, in protest, he invited his friend, Richard Beer, to stay with them in Rome for a while. Richard accepted the unexpected, generous invitation with pleasure. Being a sport pilot, he used his excellent connections at the Amsterdam Airport to swing a ticket to Rome in spite of the full Easter holiday flights. Therefore, he arrived at the airport in Rome on Monday of Holy Week, where Greg was waiting to drive him to their home. From that moment, Greg only paid attention to Richard, and only bothered to talk to Lory to ask for a drink or food.

Greg and Richard decided to connect two computers to play a strategy game. Lory was disgusted with how infantile the two men could be. She was surprised especially by Richard, who instead of visiting the Eternal City with Greg as his personal guide, wanted to play video games in a dark room. But, she didn't say anything, continuing with her housework.

With tickets provided to the Embassy, Lory participated in Easter celebrations at the Vatican: Holy Thursday in San Giovanni in Laterano, Good Friday in Via Crucis, Easter Eve mass of the resurrection, and finally the Urbi et Orbi Easter Sunday in St. Peter Square. On Pasquetta, also known as Angel's Monday, the guys organized an excursion to Anzio by the sea, and invited Lory to join them. At the end of a long walk on the beach, they had an excellent lunch at Lory's favorite restaurant, the Osteria Antica. Tuesday, Richard returned to Amsterdam, so Lory was once again able to focus on Greg, who was visibly saddened by the departure of his friend, probably because he would not have to once again deal with everyday intimacy with his wife, Lory thought.

Meanwhile Lory's friends Lilly Gruber and Marco Cocco had a baby. They were living in the charming small town of Fano on the Adriatic coast. Lory decided to visit the baby the next weekend. In addition to meeting the baby, Lory thought it might be constructive for her husband see how another family lived in the perfect harmony. Greg agreed to accompany her and they bought the presents for tiny Claudio and his parents. They left Friday at noon and arrived at the end of the motorway at via Salaria, which led them directly to Fano.

During the drive, Greg began philosophizing about the emotions generated by the birth of a baby for both the baby and its parents. He expounded on his theory that every man's most enduring desire is to return to the safety of his mother's womb. These thoughts led him to ask, or rather inform, Lory that this would be the perfect occasion to ask Lilly for some breast milk because he had forgotten its taste and was longing for it.

Lory was completely stunned. A number of thoughts ran through her head in rapid succession. She might not have minded if her husband had asked for her breast milk, but was angered that he would ask for the breast milk of another woman. She realized suddenly, she was not unique and special to Greg, but just one of the many women in the world. It quickly dawned on her just how religious and moral people in this part of Italy, the Mezzadria territory, were, and just how impolite and perverted Greg's request for mother's milk would be to them. It would destroy her friendship with Lilly, and Marco would quite literally kick Greg out of their home. Lory would also have to bear their shame and contempt for putting up with a man like Greg. She spoke up with steely determination.

"Greg, if you ask Lilly for her breast milk, I will divorce you. Remember that, because I am bloody serious."

"Okay...all right, as you wish. I didn't realize it would be that big of a deal."

"What? I **am not** in the mood to talk about this anymore."

Despite this episode, the weekend visit to see the baby was lovely. Tiny Claudio was splendid and Lory had lots of time to lot with Lilly, which deepen their friendship. Meanwhile Marco played a tennis match against Greg and defeated him, pleasing Lory. Sunday, after lunch with the new parents at an excellent restaurant, Lory and Greg left for Rome. During the long drive, they barely exchanged a word, except for some stilted statements about the landscape and the weather. Lory finally realize just the seriousness of blackmailing Greg with divorce and what it might mean for her marriage. She saw clearly that Greg had forced her hand and she was convinced it was absolutely right to push back. It would continue to be a struggle with Greg and she had to draw the line somewhere. It also became evident that her harsh words, forced by Greg's behavior, were honest, and she was heartbroken. When they arrived home, they brought up their bags without saying a word to each other. Greg sat down in front of his computer to play a game and some hours later, as if nothing had happened, he asked Lory what would they have for dinner.

CHAPTER THIRTEEN

Summer Holidays at Home

In the following days it became evident that Greg lived for the moment and forgot his words the moment he pronounced them. This made Lory's situation a little easier, because Greg seemed to forgotten what passed between them on the way to Fano. He planned their next excursion with great enthusiasm. Their next social obligation was to visit Greg's witness, Joseph, his wife Andrea, and their new born baby. Lory could not tale leave for the summer holiday until late June, so, they arrived in Amsterdam on the 28th and went to see the baby right away on Saturday, the 29th. It really felt like home visiting their old friends, since they'd been friends back in the early days of Lory and Greg's re-lationship, before Greg had left for Rome. Back then, they had played cards, enjoying each other, relaxing and laughing togeth-er many evenings. Andrea immediately offered them drinks and introduced them to the small newborn, Christopher. Lory and Greg admired him, praised him and then sat back on the sofa. Greg broke the silence.

"Joseph and Andy, may I ask you for some of Andy's breast milk? I'm eager to taste it!"

The atmosphere froze and Lory felt shocked. Joseph saved the situation with his calm reaction after taking a glance at Lory.

"Why not? Mom could you bring some of your milk to him?" he asked his wife evenly.

"I have some in the fridge." She brought some out to Greg, who drank it at once.

"Well, how was it?" Joseph asked. "Does it taste like you ex-pected it to?"

"It tastes good, but too concentrated."

Lory stood up and went with Andy to bath little Christopher. Nobody mentioned breast milk the rest of the evening. Lory knew her love for Greg was completely shattered, but the thought of divorce frightened her. Getting divorced after only one year of marriage would be absurd, she thought to herself. Her parents would blame her saying that she hadn't done enough to save her marriage, which might be true. Although her brother might understand, she figured. Andy felt her tension and decided not to say anything, speaking only to the baby.

Lory and Greg didn't speak during their drive home. Lory was unsure what to do. Should she discuss the pain she was feeling or stay silent and try to forget about it? Finally, she decided on the latter course of action and said nothing. She was surprised that Greg didn't seem to feel any embarrassment and that it never dawned on him that the ultimatum she gave him in Fano applied to all breast milk, not just Lilly's. Lory couldn't think about anything but her broken dreams. She was not unique and beloved by her husband as she imagined before their trip.

When they arrived home, Greg behaved as if nothing had happened. He was happy and natural during the following days, as well. He went to the gym with Lory, to have pizza with their friends, and he even accompanied Lory to do the shopping. Then he came up with the idea of spending a month of the summer holidays in the Canary Islands with his gay friend, Leslie. Leslie's relatives owed two apartments in a large luxurious hotel on the Island of Tenerife. Greg was so enthusiastic about the idea that he left Lory no option to decline. So, in the end, still believing in the possibility of their love, she agreed to go. She sincerely hoped that such an exotic, tropical, and romantic place might bring them closer.

Greg and Leslie organized the entire trip. To prepare, Greg and Lory purchased new clothes, toiletries, and travel guides, and got their vaccinations. Tenerife had become so popular that KLM had charter flights available. They took one of these, which was overheated, crowded and offered so little leg room that they could barely move. They made it through the uncomfortable flight, taking frequent trips to the restroom to freshen up, but having lost their sense of humor.

CHAPTER FOURTEEN

Tenerife

They landed a little before midnight at Los Rodeos airport, the only airport on Tenerife, near the city of Santa Cruz de Tenerife and took a taxi more than one hundred kilometers south to the little town of Playa de las Amercias. Keys to their apartment, in one of the best hotels, awaited their arrival. Greg and Lory were to stay in the apartment on the sixth floor, while Leslie's would stay on the tenth. The two apartments were identical, except for some personal objects and decorations left by Leslie's relatives. Since they arrived in the middle of the night they showered and went to bed immediately.

The next day, they had breakfast in the hotel and hired two umbrellas and three deck-chairs on a nearby beach. There, they mostly rested, occasionally going into the ocean for a swim. At noon they returned to the hotel for lunch, and after a short nap went to a large supermarket to buy food for the following days to avoid the cost of meals at the hotel. Each apartment was its own household. They made dinner that evening together and ate on the terrace of Leslie's apartment admiring the breathtaking view. Afterward, Leslie went out to the discos looking for around new friends and adventures, while Lory and Greg went for a walk along the beach admiring not only the ocean sunset, but also the hotel's lovely gardens and pools. Taking advantage of the romantic situation, Lory tried to nestle closer to her husband, but Greg pushed her away gently and kept a safe distance from her. So, they took their walk side by side like siblings. In fact, they spent the next two days like friends making plans for various outings.

One day, Greg took Lory shopping for clothes and perfume, which made her feel loved again. After the shopping trip, Lory's hope of possible intimacy was confirmed by Greg's behavior. He began to kiss her and made love to his wife as passionately, as he had the last time, half a year before. Lory was incredibly happy, since they spent the whole day in bed. Then they prepared dinner and brought it to Leslie's apartment. Leslie, sensing the change in their demeanor kept kidding them, saying that he knew they had made love. Lory turned red with embarrassment while Greg suggested that it was none of his business.

The next day they decided to go for a ride, taking the car left at the hotel by Leslie's relatives. It was an awfully run down Fiat 1000, with an intense smell of cat urine. They all grabbed rubber gloves and cleaning sprays and attempted to tidy up the car. They finished at noon, so, they went to their apartments for lunch and then relaxed by the hotel's swimming pool, being too tired to go to the beach. However, since they had already cleaned up the car, they decided to start discovering the island over the next few days. First, they visited the peak the Teide volcanic mountain, 3,718 meters above sea level, and admired its unique landscape and flora.

The following day they went to an eco-park full of exotic plants and animals with entertaining animal acts. Wondering through the huge park they lost their sense of time and remained in the park during its closure for siesta from noon until half past four. Nobody noticed them, since they were in the most distant part, the cactus garden. It was terribly hot and they were incredibly thirsty. The sun was shining so brightly that they nearly got sunstroke, so they were extremely happy to find the abandoned bar at the end of the cactus garden. Greg ran behind the counter and and played bar tender, handing them each a coke on the rocks. Afterwards, they found the path leading to the exit. Along the way, they admired the tropical animals. When they finally reached the exit, they ended up going against the crowd that was flowing in as the park reopened, but managed to leave without being noticed. Back at the hotel, while preparing dinner, they kept laughing at all their adventures. Lory and Greg were so tired, they decided not join Leslie at the clubs, not that he missed them, as he was on patrol, looking for new friends and flirtations.

After a few days of rest at the beach, sun-bathing and swimming in the ocean, they planned another excursion. This time they decided to explore the northern part of the island. Their first stop was Icod de Los Vinos to admire a thousand year-old tree and the dwellings of native people called guanchis. They visited the banana plantations taking in the extraordinary view of the ocean from the hills. On the way home, they stopped to swim at Puerto de la Cruz beach and visited the large Lago Martinez zoo. It was just evening when they left for home. They were approximately forty kilometers from Santa Cruz de Tenerife, when their car died in the middle of the motorway and refused to restart. It was dark and they couldn't see any buildings nearby. Fortunately, they found a parking space at a fenced area a short distance from where the car died, so they pushed it there, locked it up and left it. After analyzing their situation, they decided head back to Santa Cruz on foot, walking among the oleander bushes along the path separating the traffic-lanes. About an hour into their forced march, they found a filling station with a restaurant. They purchased refreshments and used the phone to call a taxi to take them to city center, where they hoped to find accommodations for the night. They found a room for three in a lovely hotel. The next morning, they had breakfast in one of the bars in the center and then, to make the guys happy, did some sightseeing. After that, they called a taxi to take them to the broken down car. The taxi-driver also helped them find a mechanic.

But when they reached the place where they had left the car, they noticed that it was the entrance to a large bonded warehouse. The customs employees were furious with them, demanding a fee of hundreds of thousands pezetas for the imposition of having to remove the car from the entrance. Lory, fed up with the whole situation, lost control, arguing like an Italian signora. The workers froze, backed down, repaired the car, and dropped the fee. In fact, they didn't even charge for fixing the car and sent them on their way as quickly as possible. Once on the road, nobody said anything for a while. The guys were stunned by Lory's outburst and a little ashamed that they had left it to her to fix the situation. But after about a few kilometers, they began to praise Lory and the tense atmosphere faded.

When they arrived to their hotel, they immediately took showers, had a late lunch and went for a cocktail at a beachside bar. They relaxed after a round of drinks and enjoyed recounting the adventures of their excursion. They decided to stay at the beach for dinner and began looking for a restaurant. They soon found an elegant one, in front of which a female artist was drawing portraits, glazing Lory with attraction. Lory entered the restaurant quickly to avoid a possible lesbian encounter, followed by the two guys who kept joking about her escape.

The dinner was excellent. They spent the evening talking about more serious topics like the economic and social life of the Canary Islands. Greg couldn't help kidding Leslie for his dissolute life. He took Lory's hand and said he was incredibly happy to have a wife like her. Lory almost felt dizzy and was deeply moved by her husband's words. Once again, she became convinced she could bear every difficulty by the side of the man her heart had chosen. After dinner, Leslie threw himself into the bohemian night life, while Greg and Lory went back to the apartment. Lory anticipated some tenderness from Greg, after his sweet words. but he didn't even put his arm around her shoulder, like the other pairs walking the promenade. They walked side by side, once again like siblings. Still, Lory was happy with Greg's previous statement and decided that she wouldn't hurry her husband.

The next day seemed to confirm Lory's belief that her relationship with Greg had taken a turn for the better. He bestowed more attention upon her, taking photos of her in beautiful places on the island and asking her to go parasailing and jet skiing with him. Their days fell into a regular rhythm with the occasional shopping excursion, ice cream, cocktail or walk on the beach.

It was the last week of their holiday, when one day, around siesta time, they decided to escaped from the hot weather into their cool apartment. Greg suggested that Lory get some rest while he went go upstairs to chat with Leslie. Lory agreed, smiling, but after a half hour or so she decided to join the guys. Leslie's apartment had the same layout as the one Lory and Greg occupied, the main door opening onto a long corridor from which the bedroom and bathroom opened on the right. It ended in a light and spacious American style living room with kitchen and dining room at the back leading to a panoramic terrace. When Lory entered the dark corridor and took a few steps forward, she noticed that both the living room and the terrace were empty and the bedroom door was closed. Suddenly, a thought came to her mind. She stood rooted to the spot. "What if there was something more than friendship between the guys? What if she discovered that they were having a homosexual relationship?" she asked herself. She knew that Greg's behavior was very masculine in front of his parents and friends, but it she knew that he had been somewhat girlish in his childhood. Lory stood immobile in front of the bedroom with all these thoughts running through mind. She considered opening the door, but decided not to, in case she was right. What if they were together and wanted to keep their relationship a secret? Opening the door would expose them and might embarrass them. Two strong men could do anything to her to make her keep quiet. She had even read of people disappearing or having mysterious "accidents" on tropical island. Her survival instinct won out, and she turned on her heel and left the apartment as quietly as she entered.

Once back at their apartment, she began to cry bitterly. She was so deeply disappointed, she felt she had lost all her trust in Greg. Regardless of whether or not there was a sexual relationship between Greg and Leslie, she couldn't believe her husband anymore. She couldn't stop crying. Her mind was full of thoughts, primarily self-accusations. She blamed herself for having lost her trust in Greg. She was overwhelmed by the realization that nothing would ever be the same between them.

She also realized that during the rest of the holiday she should act as if nothing had changed. She mustn't show any sign of her suspicions, because it might put her in danger.

After an hour of thinking through her options, she calmed down and began to develop a plan. First, she had to irradicate all signs of her crying spell. Once she was put back in order, she received her husband with simple-minded joy. Greg seemed elated and didn't notice anything different. He asked if she would mind preparing dinner to eat in their apartment so Leslie could come downstairs and joined them. They began to prepare grilled duck with roasted potatoes. When Greg went to let some of the the heat out of the oven, it turned out he had let too much gas accumulate and it exploded with a big bang. A ball of fire rose from the oven and burnt Greg's hair in front. They managed to extinguish the fire but there was nothing they could do about the now hairless Greg. He also lost his eyebrows and the hair on his chest. After their initial fear, they laughed at Greg's misfortune while confirming that he had not burnt his skin. This was practically their farewell dinner in Tenerife, and also their last common adventure, because the next few days were spent packing suitcases and cleaning up the apartments. Still, they found time to interrupted these preparations with few hours of swimming and relaxing at the beach. The trip to home went smoothly, so they were able to relax during the flight, full of strange adventures.

CHAPTER FIFTEEN

The Summer Goes On

Once they arrived in Rome, they had little time to get acclimated, because Greg had an important duty – he was to serve as the witness at Richard Beer's, wedding. The ceremony took place on August 31st at the Hall of the City Council followed by a party in a private garden. It went well, except, once again, Greg didn't dance with Lory. His lack of interest in dancing with her at this wedding hurt her feelings again, even though she had already given up any hope of saving her marriage and was just waiting for the right time to tell Greg. Over the past few weeks, she did her best to be a good wife and didn't feel inclined to inform Greg about her suspicions in Tenerife and their impact on her decision to divorce him. Rather than spoil the happiness of Richard's wedding and the pleasure of visiting with family in Holland, she decided to wait to speak with Greg when they were back Rome, alone again. However, that would take a while, because Greg decided to give Richard a four-week long honeymoon in Italy as a wedding present.

Richard and his new bride, Christine, arrived in Rome in the second half of September, about the same time Lory and Greg returned to their Roman flat. The two couples met up directly in the castle hotel of Torre di Albidone in the Calabria region of Italy. They spent the first week together, after which Lory and Greg left the newlyweds and travelled back to Rome for a week. Then for the third and fourth weeks of the honeymoon, they rented an apartment for four in the picturesque historic center of the coastal city of Gaeta, two blocks from the port. Lory and Greg only spent weekends with the couple, travelling together to the fabulous beach in the Bay of the Water Nymphs.

The last straw for Lory was when, in Calabria, Greg rudely rejected her tender intimate approach. Lory finally made the irreversible decision to divorce him. In spite of her decision, she continued to try to act the part of a good wife during the rest of the holiday. Still, she was surprised that Greg hadn't noticed anything about her state of mind. While at the aqua-park near Sibari, Lory got fed up with Greg's childish behavior one day and asked Christine to drive her husband back to the hotel, because she was taking their car to go home, being in a rush to exit. Surprisingly Greg got the message that time and ran after her. He asked Lory to come with him to discover the beauties of one a historic town in the area, rather than going back to the hotel. Lory finally accepted his invitation, so they went together to Sibari and then to Cerchiara.

Lory continued to be amazed that her husband was so completely immune to the tension she felt, acting as if everything was all right between them, while in reality he was using Lori as cover to protect his public image as a good husband, and also having a gay lover disguised as a legitimate friendship. Lory finally understood the meaning of a remark Greg made some weeks earlier that when they had children he would never leave them alone with Leslie, because Greg could not trust him. Of course, Greg couldn't trust Leslie, since he had sex with him. Not only was she suffering from Greg's lack of love for her and the fact she was now jealous not only of other women but also of other men, but on top of that, their children would be in danger with his "friends." She realized that the last thing she wanted now was to have children with Greg. It was a nightmare for her.

However, during their visits with Richard and Christine she tried to act as though everything was OK. She went with her husband and their friends to swim in the sea, eat ice cream, have dinner and afterward she enjoyed the fabulous coastal atmosphere of the roof terrace by candle light. Having spent the weekend together, Lory and Greg went back to Rome where she could recharge, focusing on her work as a life line. She was fighting for survival in every other area of her life.

For example, during the second weekend they spent with their friends in Gaeta, Greg and Richard hired a motorboat to take their wives on a coastal sightseeing trip. They went from the Bay of the Water Nymphs to the so called "Well of the Devil," one of the most attractive natural phenomena in the world. The "well" is a flue carved by the sea into the coastal rocks with an entrance at its bottom. They wanted to enter the flue through this aperture, but it was too low for the boat. So, they anchored, dove into the sea, and entered the Well of the Devil swimming through the aperture. Inside, the water was smooth and brightly lit by the sun entering from the opening at the top. They enjoyed swimming and diving in its splendid water, which was so transparent, it didn't seem too deep. When Richard's diving mask filled with water and sunk to the sandy bottom of the flue, he swam down to grab it. He didn't realize that he had gone down four or five meters to reach it, hurting his eardrums and making him feel like they were broken.

"Well, fixing my ears will cost a lot more than the price of another diving mask." he said, annoyed at his own stupidity.

As if this wasn't unlucky enough, the guys wanted to try a stunt they had seen in a James Bond film where he was pulled by a rope behind a boat. To try it, they had to drop off their wives off. So, they left them in the sea near the rocks at the entrance of the Well of the Devil. While the guys pulled each other bound by a rope, the boat making rapid turns, the women were fighting the large waves which nearly pushed them into the rocks. They had to use all their strength to avoid getting crushed into the rocks and became angry with their husbands' irresponsibility. Lory, being a better swimmer, had to calm Christine, who was terrified of both the rocks and her struggle to breath as the wave pushed against her chest. About the time she decided risk climbing the rocks, the guys arrived to pick up their furious wives who gave them a thorough dressing-down for their irresponsible and childish behavior.

After the two weeks spent in Gaeta, Richard and Christine stayed in Rome at Lory's flat for an additional week. Once again, the guys opted to play computer games, rather than visit the sights of Rome. They struggled to reconnected two computers to play a strategy game against each other, while Lory did the ironing and Christine watched a DVD in Italian. She didn't bother with subtitles, because she had already seen the movie in Dutch. Greg came in and told them that he and Richard were headed to a computer shop on Cola di Rienzo street to buy a cable to connect the two computers.

After an hour or so, he reentered the flat, exhausted. He asked Lory, very sweetly, if she could go with him because, supposedly, only she could solve a problem with the police. Going downstairs, Lory saw that the guys had been in an accident. They went to the Cola di Rienzo street in Richard's car, but it stopped and wouldn't start again. So, they returned to the Institute on foot and took Lory's car to tow Richard's back to the Institute. When they had almost reached the Institute's gate in the Piazzale Villa Giulia, a motorcycle came flying through wanting to cut between the two cars and got tangled in the rope. The motorcyclist flew over his handlebars, but, luckily, didn't get hurt. But he didn't want to admit his responsibility. The police informed Greg and Richard that it was absolutely forbidden to pull a vehicle using a soft rope in Rome. As a result of the Lory's diplomatic intervention, the police cut the penalty for Greg and the motorcyclist in half and helped Greg and Richard take the broken down car to a mechanic's garage nearby. This childish adventure, once again confirmed that Lory couldn't continue to share her life with Greg. He had caused too many incidents. She was so unhappy that she could have cry for days and days. Meanwhile, Greg continued not to notice any sign of the problems in their relationship. He continued to kid, laugh, and act just like he had at the beginning of their relationship.

Richard's car was repaired quickly, but the guys gave up on connecting their computers. They agreed to let Lory take the lead and followed her to discover the beauties of Rome. The day of their farewell, they all got up at three o'clock and Lory drove while Richard and Christine followed in their car through the city to the right highway.

However, Richard and Christine were not Greg and Lory's last guests of the season. Greg's parents were also coming for visit. Lory and Greg developed an elaborate and very active plan for the visit, as per Greg's desire. Dave and Gabi arrived by plane, so Greg went to pick them up and bring them back to their flat. His parents were both historians and linguists by profession, so, they were enchanted simply to be in Rome, and ignored the dense and detailed program Lory and Greg had developed for their Roman holidays. First they walked around the historical center, visiting all its prominent museums. Then they went to Tivoli and admired Hadrian's Villa and the Villa d'Este. One evening, they attended a concert in Sutri in the Etruscan amphitheater. Another evening, they went to a concert at the Teatro di Marcello. Afterwards they visited Anzio, Nettuno, Tarquinia, Cerveteri, Fumone etc. and they spent a whole day in Gaeta, where after a sightseeing tour, they had an excellent lunch in an elegant and stylish restaurant in the port.

After lunch, they hired a motorboat to tour the picturesque rocky coast by water. Once they found a calm and romantic bay, they anchored, and Lory and Greg went for a swim. The water was clear and transparent. They could see the sand below, imprinted with the pattern of the waves. Lory was enchanted by the underwater world, the sun rays entering the water above and and the schools of colorful fish around her. But when she returned to the surface, she noticed that Greg was already in the boat with his parents and that it was moving away from her. She was shocked, feeling like an abandoned dog, thrown out of a car. First she panicked. Then she began to shout, but the noise of the motor was louder, so Greg's family couldn't hear her. Then the boat disappeared behind a rocky hill next to the bay. In desperation, Lory swam to the beach in the small bay. There were two villas there, with large gardens, each with a gate to the beach. Lory got out of the water and cowered on the hot sand, wearing only a bikini and her snorkeling mask. She began to cry for the hopeless of her situation. She didn't have the faintest idea why Greg's family wanted to get rid of her. After a bit, an elderly, well-built, tanned man came out of one of the villas and went to her directly asking, "Signorina, what happened? What can I do to help?"

"Thank you, but I really don't know," Lory stuttered, ashamed for having a family that left her alone in the middle of nowhere without saying a word. Finally, the man managed to draw the truth out of her.

"Signorina, let me introduce myself. My name is Tiziano Ferretti and I am at your service with my house and my car, if you need it."

"Thank you so much, you are very kind! Your kindness is really moving" Lory said in a faltering voice and let the man pull her up from the sandy ground. But as they were going toward the villa gate, the boat reappeared. Greg was shouting her name.

"My husband and my in-laws," Lory said indifferently.

"I hope you don't intend to go back to them, Signora!" Ferretti exclaimed in protest. "They don't deserve you!"

"I must go back with them. I am a member of the Dutch diplomatic staff in Rome, so I simply cannot be involved in a conflict. But, rest assured, I've decided to divorce my husband. I just have to choose the right moment to tell him. You know, we have only been married for a year."

"I understand. Nevertheless, I am pleased to have met a woman like you. You can always count on my services and can rely on me as a friend. I hope to see you again!"

"Thank you for your friendship. You are my savior and I will be always grateful for you. You can find me anytime in Rome, at the Holland Institute on via Omero under the street number 10-12."

"Then I shall see you, again!"

"That would be lovely. Good-bye!" Lory said whole-hearted. Then she dove into the sea and swam toward the boat on which Greg was standing and waving to her.

After she got into the boat the atmosphere grew icy. Lory lay flat on her stomach on the wooden deck with her back to Greg and his parents. At first, Greg first tried chatting her up, but without success. So, they sailed back to Gaeta in tense silence.

When they arrived at the port they had built up so much momentum that the boat entered at a very high speed. All those in the water, mainly divers, dropped what they were doing and ran, hand in hand, to the break water. They began to shout, giving instructions to Dave to avoid impact, so as not to destroy the boat. Finally, Greg grabbed the wheel from his father and put the boat in reverse, slowing down enough to glide into the mooring. Lory, not only angry, but terrified as well, jumped out of the boat and ran to get dressed. Greg followed her and tried to convince her to go back to the boat. Dave was upset and wanted to make up for the incident by hiring the boat for another few hours, demonstrating his ability to drive it. Lory refused the idea, but Greg began to beg her to forgive his father's actions, and she started to think through the situation. It was clear that she had to go back to Rome with them in the same car and had to bear them for another week in her flat, so she finally accepted the apology and went back to the boat with Greg.

This time Dave thanked her for her return with a light smile and started to cross the bay, sailing toward the town of Formia. But he hadn't calculated the distance well, so Formia was much farther away than it seemed. It was late afternoon and they were all still wearing wet swim suits. Lory and Gabi wrapped themselves in their towels against the cold wind. By sun set, having reached the middle of the bay, they all struggled with the cold winds on the open sea. Greg gathered all his courage and began to persuade his father to turn back to Gaeta. Eventually, Dave agreed and took them back. They got dressed and went to dinner in an elegant restaurant. While enjoying a lovely meal, all of them, except Lory, rediscovered their sense of humor. Since Lory was the only one who didn't drink wine that evening, she had to drive them back to Rome, where they arrived around midnight.

The next morning, after her usual preparations, Lory went to her office in a hurry to avoid her in-laws and her husband. At noon she had no choice but to meet them for lunch at her flat. Lory made a frosted sofficini findus and tried to block out their irritating conversation. Greg and his parents were laughing at their adventures in Gaeta, which Lory did not find at all amusing. She needed to talk to someone about her pain. So, she went back to her office to call her god parents without being interrupted. Her godfather, Carlo, answered the phone and when he began to speak with his wise, calm voice, greeting her with love and joy, Lory could no longer hold back. She started to cry. Carlo tried to soothe her and asked her to tell him everything. Then, he suggested that she visit them in Camogli as soon as possible. She had been to the picturesque small city situated in Liguria many times. It always felt like being in a fairy tale. Her godparents were very happy and proud of her when she was selected for cultural diplomatic work in Rome, and they promised her parents to take care of her during her mission in Italy. They had come to see her once in Rome, surprising her colleagues, who were unaware of Lory's personal Italian relationships. Carlos was an old friend of her father ever since them met at a conference in Italy. Their friendship extended to their wives, Giussy and Helen. They all felt deep mutual care and affection for each other. Lory wanted to visit her god parents, since they were the first people to whom she had spoken of her unhappy marriage. However, because she had already exhausted her leave, she had no choice but to share her anxiety with Giussy and Carlo by phone. They understood her difficult situation and stood by her with understanding, discretion and helpfulness.

After her in-laws left for Japan, Lory and Greg continued their usual, "normal" and "harmonious" life. By then, it was the middle of October and the academic year had begun for Greg, so he became very busy.

CHAPTER SIXTEEN

The Right Time

Returning to their everyday routine didn't solve the problem of Greg's ambiguity, bi-sexuality at best, homosexuality more likely. Lory had made her decision. She was just waiting for the right time to tell her husband in order not to disrupt her work and diplomatic status. She knew that her decision would cause deep tensions not only for Greg but also for their parents who had become close friends. Lory's marriage seemed perfect to them, since her husband treated her like a princess and heaped kindness and presents on her. Only Lory knew the truth. Finally, she decided that the next weekend would be the right time to talk to Greg about their marriage. But just as she prepared to confront him, he arranged a short holiday to Venice, stopping along the way to visit Lilli and Marco in Fano to see how Claudio had grown. They left Friday after lunch and arrived in Fano in the afternoon. They spent only a couple of hours with Lilli and her family and then drove directly to Venice, where they left the car in the huge parking structure and continued on their way by water taxi.

It was almost dinner time when they arrived at the five-star Hotel Baglioni, where Greg had booked a room for them with a view of Saint Mark's Square. The hotel was luxurious, magnificent and splendid, just like the city itself. Lory was incredibly happy with Greg's generous arrangements and with the special attention he was paying to her. Somewhere deep in her heart, she still wanted to trust Greg every time he behaved this way.

After taking possession of their room, they went to dinner in a romantic medieval restaurant. Later that evening, they took a long walk in the "calles" and canals of the Venice. Lory was still willing to give a Greg a chance, if he could express his sincere love for and only her, in spite of his sexual orientation. She wanted to be the only real relationship in his life. She also hoped Greg would express his love in a romantic way in the city of love, maybe with a "stolen" kiss in the dark and empty streets of Venice and a weekend filled with the kind of love that suited the place. However, Greg made no gestures while they were walking in the abandoned streets after their first dinner in Venice, nor during the night. He only wanted to talk about arts and history, and when they returned to their hotel room he switched on the TV and almost immediately fell asleep watching it.

The next morning, they had an abundant, early breakfast in the huge, medieval dining room of the hotel, after which they went for a walk in the city. Greg hired a gondola and they went for a long sightseeing tour. It seemed likely that he planned to rekindle their relationship. Perhaps he did understand Lory's disappointment and the widening gap between them.

Everything went as Lory had hoped. When they reached the Bridge of Sighs, Greg kissed her while they passed under the bridge. Then, he put his arm around his wife. But Lory was not satisfied with the kiss. It felt like a duty completed, without passion. Lory felt conflicting emotions, the beauty of the gondola tour and the disappointment of their waning love. The rest of the day strengthened her disappointment. The most intimate Greg became was to suggest they play the Venetian version of the Lara Croft computer game they used to play together. It wasn't enough. She no longer wanted to have baby with Greg and had to admit to herself that they were past any possibility of repairing their relation and their marriage. She was sorry to lose the luxurious life she could live with Greg, but to keep it, she would have had to renounce her soul, which just wasn't worth it. As a member of the Catholic community in Maastricht, she had absorbed real Catholic values and couldn't see herself entering into a pact with devil for creature comfort. She also realized that she didn't want to visit the most beautiful places in the world as part of an emotionally empty marriage, feeling constant pain of the frustration. For the first time, she was happy the she and Greg only had a civil marriage ceremony, without an oath of eternal faith in front of God.

The following evening was as dull as the previous, all form but no feeling. They went to dinner in a romantic and rustic medieval restaurant where all the other guests were cheerfully talking to their companions. Only Lory and Greg sat side by side without saying a word. In that restaurant, Lory realized how large the gap between her and her husband had become. They had nothing to say to each other. Greg still seemed to believe he could repair their relationship which, due to him, was irremediable. Lory resigned herself to their impending divorce, which was was now inevitable. After dinner they spent their evening watching TV and went to sleep early.

The next morning Greg woke up, acting as if everything was all right. They went downstairs to breakfast, checked out, and returned to their room to pack and leave by ten o'clock. On their way home Greg drove while Lory enjoyed the beauty of the Italian landscape, thinking of the possibility of finding real love in her future, the love that her parents and some of her friends had. She wished for a spouse with whom could share the wonderful experiences and impressions she had visiting the most famous parts of the world.

Arriving home, Lory got out of the car and threw herself into housework, which she found comforting. Then she called Nick to get updated on the happenings of the weekend. Finally, she phoned Phil to schedule their upcoming art history lessons. She realized that she could only bear her ruined marriage here in Rome, surrounded by her everyday life. It was only in Rome that she could mend broken pieces of her heart.

CHAPTER SEVENTEEN

The Milestone

Since the week-end in the city of love did not improve anything in her marriage, Lory had to pick another date to tell her husband that things between them couldn't go on this way any longer and that she did not see any solution to their problems. She decided to start the conversation one evening after dinner. She tried to focus on their lack of intimacy, emphasizing that neither of them was truly happy. But Greg did not agree that the situation was irredeemable. He kept repeating that he was still in love with Lory, but had spent so much time in Japan on his own that he got used to a lack of intimacy which is why he couldn't express his emotions. Lory no longer accepted this argument. Earlier in their marriage she was willing to believe his excuses. But by now, she felt the facts provide that this was only a cover story to hide Greg's ambiguity and predisposition to homosexuality.

Nevertheless, taking Greg's emotions into account, especially because he became so angry he had just broken the bed, Lory tried to avoid an argument. To her surprise, he came up with a new excuse, saying that he avoided intimacy with Lory to test himself to see if he could resist temptation, so he could remain faithful to his wife when she became pregnant someday. He begged for a year of probation during which he could demonstrate his love and passion for Lory.

The next day, Greg came up with one of his typical ideas, suggesting they spend the winter after Christmas in Andalusia with his sister Angelique and her family. Lory accepted the invitation, willing to bear another holiday for the sake of their marriage.

Her soul kept whispering to get out of her marriage as soon as possible, but her brain reminded her how inconsiderate it was to only give one year to see if a marriage could work. Since their parents had become close friends, a divorce would impact them as well. Lory was afraid to cause so much pain. She didn't know what she had hoped when she accepted Greg's request of a probation period. Maybe she was waiting for some kind of miracle, so he could return the same feelings she felt in her heart at the beginning of what seemed to be a fairy tale.

The weeks and months passed quickly, but their relationship didn't improve. One afternoon in November, Lory entering the bathroom, found her husband masturbating. This made her so angry that she started crying and shouting at Greg, asking him why he excluded her from his intimacy, his desires, and his dreams. Greg was ashamed, but there was nothing he could say to defend himself. Lory realized this was another milestone in her life of adversity and alienation.

Meanwhile, Phil and Anna reached their own milestone. Anna had left in September to begin a year of studies specializing in zoology in Barcelona. Phil told Lory that they had agreed to keep in touch by phone and Skype until Christmas. Then Anna would come home for the holidays, and, in the spring, Phil would go to Barcelona to visit Anna. During their art history lessons, Phil couldn't help asking Lory for advice about how to make a long distance relationship work. So, they didn't spend much time on art. Lory kept her marriage problems secret from everyone, including Phil. One evening after their lesson Anna, called Lory from Barcelona.

"Hi Lory! It's Anna in Barcelona," the excited girl started the conversation.

"Hi Anna! What's new? How are you?"

"I'm so sorry for disturbing you, but you are the only person I can turn to. I don't think anyone else would understand my situation."

"What situation? Please calm down and tell me what's going on."

"I'm pregnant. Can you imagine? It must have happened the last time Phil and I were together, since he's the only man in my life."

"I know. Don't worry. We will figure this out! How far along are you?"

"I'm in the third month, so it must have happened at the beginning of September."

"I see, Anna. Have you told anyone else?"

"No, I don't dare. Nobody knows, except you."

"I think you need to talk to Phil about this. I'm sure he'll understand. But don't say a word to your parents, yet, at least until you return home for Christmas. I'm sure they will accept your baby with joy because of their faith. You do want keep the baby, don't you?"

"Of course, I do! But I'm so afraid. Phil and I haven't made any serious plans."

"Phil told me last winter that he wanted to propose to you. He wants a future with you. You can rely on him, I'm sure of it!"

"Really? Are you sure?"

"Yes, I am. He asked me for advice and I told him that it was clear you two have a real love, the kind that can resist all kinds of obstacles, so, you don't have to be in a hurry. A love like yours will only get stronger as time passes."

"Thank you for sharing all this. So, you think I should talk to him?"

"Absolutely, yes! Don't exclude him from such an important moment in your life and your common future! It matters to both of you. The sooner you talk to him, the better it will be. If I were you, I would call him this very evening. Cheer up and be brave! You'll see, it will be alright."

"I am so grateful for your advice! Thank you so much. I will call him this evening."

"Good! Hugs, and kisses! Good-bye!"

"Many hugs and kisses to you, too. Thank you. Bye-bye!" Anna put down the receiver. Lory remained immobile in her armchair in the dark living room, absorbed in thought. She was thinking about the challenging situation her young friends were facing and had to admit that this moment was a milestone not only for her and Greg, but also for Anna and Phil.

CHAPTER EIGHTEEN

Difficulties in Wintertime

Lory installed an autumn exhibit at the Institute, dedicated to Dutch contemporary artists. There were so many artists that she had to organize a second session to exhibit them all. The second session was set to open at Christmas. For this occasion, Lory also organized an international conference with the title "Space and Form in Contemporary Art", providing an excellent way to start the new year, as well. Veltmann loved the idea and was very proud of how it would impact their stature among the other institutes and academies. He didn't have the faintest idea about the real reason she organized the conference and gave him such a prominent role – Lory intended to make the Director happy professionally so he would be in the best possible mood to accept the news about Anna's pregnancy and his son's fatherhood. There were only a few days left to Christmas, and Anna and Phil were eager to announce their news. Lory, despite her own miserable private life, became their primary confidential supporter, protector, and adviser. Lory knew that Anna and Phil's love was heaven sent, something their parents did not yet understand, since they had not yet had the opportunity to see it themselves.

The exhibition, with the same title as the conference, opened on December 23rd, the same day Anna arrived. Her plane landed at noon and Lory and Phil went to pick her up at the airport. When they arrived at Anna's parents' home, Lory and Phil brought in her bags, positioning themselves to cover Anna's growing belly. Phil, following Lory's advice, took the hands of his future mother and father-in-law and asked for Anna's hand. The parents stepped back in surprise, but they couldn't hide their happy smiles. However, their smiles disappeared when Lory and Phil let them see Anna while Phil announced. "We have joyful news for you. We are going to have a baby!"

Luciano and his wife, Marta de Angelis both sat back down quickly in their armchairs and asked the youngsters to stand in front of them. Lory's presence was useful to the young couple, because it constrained how Anna's parents spoke to their daughter and future son-in-law, choosing their word carefully. Lory stayed with them during the whole conversation, in spite of her need to go back to the Institute to deal with the opening ceremony of the next exhibition. Luckily, Anna's parents quickly accepted her pregnancy. When Phil voiced worries about how his parent might react, they came up with an interesting idea.

"Why don't you get married before talking to your parents about the baby? If you do, your parents will have to accept you as a real family, waiting for a legitimate baby," Marta suggested while her husband nodded his approval.

"It's a great idea and it can work," Lory added, encouraging the youngsters. "Phil, your parents already know Anna and have accepted your relationship. So, you will only be strengthening it, by making it official. You already intended to propose Anna, before the baby. Well, it's time you got married as soon as possible! Marta's right. It will be better not to mention the baby just yet. Your parents will be very busy with the exhibition and international conference I've planned. Once they hear your news, it will make them happy that their son is has take responsibility and made a serious decision, like a real adult."

"I totally agree," Marta stated, and added, "even though Phil is a Lutheran, the two of you could get married in the Catholic Church, because marriage is now permitted between the denominations, as long as the baby is baptized a Christian. If you agree, we can contact Don Giorgio, the priest at the church Santa Maria in Trastevere. We belong to his community and he can take care of everything. Luciano and I got married in that church, as well."

"This is all great news and very comforting to hear," Phil declared with joy. "My dear," he turned to Anna, "you see, everything will be all right. No need to worry! Also, I don't think it's a good idea for you of the baby to return to Barcelona for your second semester. It could endanger both your health."

"What can I say, I have to agree," Marta chimed in supporting her future son-in-law. "Here at home, we are available to help in case of an emergency, which I hope we can avoid."

"All right. You are right. I'm convinced," Anna accepted the counsel of her loved ones. "I will not go back to Barcelona. I will ask a friend to send my belongings back here."

"Then it's decided. Marta can start to plan the wedding with Don Giorgio. And you, Anna, must avoid the Institute. Phil's parents cannot become aware of your state, yet. Phil can come to see you every day or so and demonstrate to his parents how important this relationship is for him," Lory summarized in a peremptory tone. "And now, Phil, we need to head back to the Institute. I have a lot of work to do, with the opening ceremony of our current exhibit this evening. Say good-bye to Anna, but hurry up. I'll be waiting for you in the car."

The opening ceremony of the exhibition went smoothly and was a great success, attracting a new crowd to the Institute. One advantage of holding a contemporary art exhibition, is that all the relatives and friends of the exhibiting artists come to the opening ceremony to take part in the artists' success. Unknown contemporary artists come to these events, too, in hopes of meeting an important art critic and getting discovered. Rich people often visit these events to show their knowledge and wealth, and sometimes to invest in the truly awful works that have been declared valuable by a known art critic. Finally, many art experts also attend. All were in attendance that evening.

As always, the opening ceremony was followed with a reception. The tables were laid with fine food, but were unreachable due to the size of the the crowd. Lory seldom ate at these events because she was always busy socializing. She typically put a nice salty appetizer on her plate while mingling with VIP guests, wanting to ensure that her every action reflected well on the Institute and the Director.

The reception ran late, and Lory, exhausted but satisfied, took a shower went to bed. Anna and Phil's secret marriage was the greatest adventure of her life, so she couldn't think of anything else before falling asleep. She was worried about the possibility of Phil's parents discovering the secret over the Christmas holidays when they would be spending more time with their son.

The next morning, it felt strange to wake up beside Greg. Lory had been so focused on Anna and Phil, that she had her pushed her own situation and problems from her mind. Greg couldn't stand contemporary art and expressed his negative attitude publicly, so Lory was very happy that he had not attended the event. After breakfast together, they got ready in hurry, said farewell and went to work. December 24th, the Vigilia and Christmas Eve, was a regular working day in Italy, allowing people to clear their desks before taking off for the Holidays. Greg had lost of students who needed to take exams, while Lory had to arrange the last details of the international conference. All the speakers and the time of their presentations had just been confirmed and their travel and lodgings arranged. She only needed to finalize and print the conference's program and posters. After that, she could concentrate all her attention on Anna and Phil.

Meanwhile, Father Leonardo agreed to hold the wedding on December 27th at 10 o'clock. Now that the wedding date was settled, Lory began to arrange her personal plans so that she could participate in the ceremony without raising suspicion or being waylaid by Greg. She told him that she would meet her friends Cecilia and Elisabetta on December 27th to look for party dresses for the New Year's Eve ball. She also arranged to keep Phil's parents busy with the conference. Lory wrote up the text for Veltmann's speeches, so the Director would have time to learn them and recite them by memory. No one questioned the fact that Phil planned to spend the holidays with Anna's family.

Christmas Eve dinner, arranged by the Veltmanns proceeded as usual, with almost all Institute employees in attendance, except for Nick, who decided to spend the winter holidays at home in the Netherlands. He planned to come back in time for the conference, the first event of the new year. Since he would be gone anyways, Lory and Phil decided not to share their secret with him. Meanwhile, Lory took every occasion to praise Phil's maturity, intellect, ambition, reliability and independence to the Veltmanns. She was careful not to overdo it, though, to avoid raising suspicion.

After the dinner, Lory made a point of updating Phil about his parents' mood. She was eager to support the wedding. There were still three days left until the ceremony. Lory spent them by Veltmann's side, keeping him occupied with the details of the conference. Fortunately, he liked being engaged in the planning and added ideas that enhanced the program. Everything was proceeding according to plan for Lory and her protected young lovers.

The Secret Marriage

Typically, one of the most challenging parts of planning a wedding is the agreeing on the invitation list and the seating plan. But in this case, the challenge was just the opposite – how to keep the wedding absolutely secret. When the big day arrived, Lory tried to extricate herself from the conference without raising Veltmann's suspicion. She decided to use the same white lie she had told Greg, that she had to go and deal with her New Year's Eve party dress.

In the Church of Santa Maria in Trastevere, in front of Father Leonardo, only the spouses, Anna's parents and grandparents, who couldn't be left out of such an important event, the witnesses, Lory and Anna's best friend Teresa, and Teresa's husband, Luca, were present. The ceremony was short and simple, but also very romantic as Anna and Phil sealed their union for the rest of their lives. Lory and Teresa signed the marriage certificate. In spite of their worries, nervousness and heightened emotions, Lory had never seen a happier couple in her life. Anna wore a long, simple white silk dress, pleated under her breast. She didn't need a luxurious designer wedding dress to be the most beautiful bride in the world. Lory's heart was deeply moved by the scene and the sermon Father Leonardo gave. After the ceremony, Marta invited all of them for lunch at the splendid Il Cavolo (the Cabbage) restaurant situated outside the GRA, Rome's ring road, along the Via Appia road. Lory always liked the place, which is situated on a hill of the Castelli Romani, before the city of Grottaferrata, where the road divides. The owner was very busy, dealing with the kitchen and the guests all by himself, while treating his guests with great hospitality, making suggestions for their meal choices. The restaurant was perfect for a romantic and elegant wedding reception.

Marta had managed to booked a large table at the last minute. The table was covered by a large, white, damask table cloth with a floral runner that stretched the length of the table. The plates, water, wine and champagne glasses were placed carefully along the colorful floral runner at the perfect distance from each other. Glass vases filled with roses and a big antique vase full of splendid flowers completed the table setting. Marta had even managed to prepare a seating plan, providing each guest with name card at their place at the table and a small bunch of lavender, a lovely memento of the event.

Lory knew that she couldn't stay for the entire event. Her long absence from the Institute would create suspicion. So, she congratulated the new couple, gave them her wedding present, and told them that she couldn't stay for more than two hours.

"We understand," Phil and Anna responded together at the same time, "and we are so grateful for all your help. We will never forget the huge role you played in our wedding! We're happy that you can celebrate with us at least for another two hours! Enjoy yourself."

"It was a pleasure to help you and I'm extremely happy to have been able to take part in the fulfilment of your love," Lory answered and went to her place at the table.

The lunch was a la carte, so they could choose what they wanted to eat from the menu. Lory selected sweet melon with Parma ham for the appetizer, then a a linguine with truffle, and for the main course a steak with grilled vegetables. To complete the lunch, she had an espresso, then she said good-bye. Anna offer her a piece of cake to take with her, which Lory had to decline. "I won't be able to explain that to Greg," she said.

"You can tell him you bought it at a confectioner. We'll wrap it in the original wrapping paper from the bakery to avoid any suspicion. Or, better yet, you don't have to tell him anything.

Phil can bring it to you saying it was left over from Christmas dinner."

"All right, that will work." They hugged and said good-bye.

Lory got in her car and drove back to the institute in hurry. She arrived back just in time, before anyone noticed her absence.

CHAPTER TWENTY

The New Year Eve

As always, the Holland Institute celebrated New Year's Eve by holding a ball for all its employees and their families. Veltmann made sure to invite everybody as was their tradition. It would have been odd for Phil to miss it, or to attend without Anna, so it was time to share the truth about their marriage and the baby. The Veltmanns were openminded and tolerant, but Phil still worried about whether the news might upset them. He and Anna had only one day left to prepare themselves, with Lory's help, to make their announcement.

On the morning of December 30th, Lory went to Anna's family home using the excuse that she needed a final fitting for her party dress. This was only a partial lie, since Marta worked as a dressmaker for Cinecittá, a large film studio in Rome, and had actually made a new party dress for Lory. Together, they all came up with a strategy to present their secret. On the 31st after the Veltmanns had had time to get up and prepared for the day, Phil would bring Anna to the Institute where Lory would join them. Together they would go to the residence and announce their news so Phil and Anna could share their joy in person.

Once Phil and Anna arrived, Phil went to speak to his parent alone. Having carefully chosen his words, he began.

"Mom and dad, you know that I and Anna have been together for more than a year and that I love her very much. Well, I want to let you know that we decided to get married."

"Isn't it a bit soon? You're still attending secondary school, my dear," Ingrid Veltmann replied.

"Your mother is right, my son. Marriage is an important step in life and must be carefully thought through to avoid making a mistake," Paul Veltmann added.

"Please, let me explain this better. I've wanted to marry Anna for a very long time now. I told Lory, but she persuaded me to wait, raising the same concerns you have just now. But now, Anna and I are expecting a baby. So, we decided to get married."

He went to the door and opened it asking Anna and Lory to come in. The Veltmanns were standing in the middle of the room, eyes wide-open, stunned. They couldn't help gazing at Anna's belly, while she greeted her new in-laws politely. An embarrassing silence followed. Finally, Phil spoke up.

"We've decided to do this ourselves and no one can separate us. We want this baby and we've gotten married. We just hope you will accept it share our happiness."

"How could you leave us out of your big day? We missed the wedding of our only son!" Ingrid cried, clearly upset.

"How can you worry about missing a wedding when our son has just destroyed his career?" Paul responded to his wife.

"Come on, daddy! I haven't destroyed anything. I can and will continue to build my career. After finishing secondary school, I will enroll at the University of Studies 'La Sapienza' in the school of Archeology and History of Art, which you know is the best in the field. And, because we haven't yet held a civil wedding ceremony we can still celebrate together, especially if mom would help organize it."

"Of course. We will rent the ceremonial hall of the Capitolium and will throw a magnificent reception afterwards! You can count on me to manage all the details. So, tell us about your wedding," She kissed her son on the cheeks, and extended a hand to Anna.

Lory was pleased that she didn't have to say a word. It was good to know that the young couple had managed this difficult conversation without her help. However, Veltmann was not ready to let her go.

"I suppose you knew about all of this?"

"Yes, Signor Director. But it would have been impossible to change the facts and, thank God, their love is sincere. They've always been solid in their esteem for each other, especially as they worked through these difficult times. I only helped make their way a little smoother."

"Thank you, Lory. We are forever obligated to you. Right, dear?" Ingrid said to Lory, eying her husband.

"Yes, of course. Thank you Dottoressa Hennes," Paul responded, under pressure from his wife, with a note of surrendered in his voice.

So, the New Year's Eve ball started with the Veltmann family having weathered their most recent storm. The Institute staff gathered in the huge living room in the residence to say farewell to the previous year. They commenced to dance and enjoy the buffet that the Veltmanns provided. Meanwhile, Lory returned to her own private crisis. Her significant role helping Anna and Phil distracted her from her own woes and no one suspected just how unhappy she was. Now that the Veltmanns had learned of their son's situation and accepted it, she had to deal with her own problems. Greg still hadn't seemed to notice Lory's inner conflict, much less the secrets she'd kept over the last week. He was cheerfully talking and joking with those around him, in typical Greg style. When he asked Lory to dance, she felt she had to say yes, but her was heart full of pain, wondering what she was doing in the arms of a man who used her to disguise his sexual orientation from the world. She felt so awful she almost began to cry right there, but held back her tears so her husband could enjoy this moment in happy ignorance.

CHAPTER TWENTY-ONE

The Conference and the Crisis

After the winter holidays, all employees at the Institute concentrated on the conference. There was a lot to do with the arrival of the speakers and guests. Lory ran the show, although, officially, Veltmann was in charge. To Lory, the entire Institute, including the receptionist and caretaker, felt like an agitated buzzing beehive. Lory received the guests and arranged their accommodations, providing each with a copy of the official program. The next morning the first presentations took place. Lory waited anxiously for her first coffee break to give Nick, who for some mysterious reason hadn't arrived back from his holidays, a call. She managed to reach him at the Amsterdam airport on his way back to Rome. He planned to arrive later that the afternoon. Lory promised to send Gigi to the Fiumicino Airport to pick him up and returned to the conference.

The conference theme attracted huge interest, since Rome is one of the greatest centers of the artistic world. Lory enjoyed the presentations as well as the deep and thoughtful questions participants put to the speakers. To her, it demonstrated the importance of the conference.

She had almost forgotten about her personal misery, when Nick arrived and informed her about his engagement to Caroline, his former girlfriend from secondary school. It was too much for Lory. She ran straight to her flat, dropped down on her bed, and began crying bitterly. Nick, surprised by Lory's reaction and sudden departure, began to look for ways to be useful at the conference. As the afternoon coffee break approached, Veltmann found Nick and asked if knew where Lory was, since Gigi had seen her last speaking to him. Veltmann needed Lory's help as soon as possible and sent Nick to find her. Nick hadn't the faintest idea where to start. First, he went to the ladies' room, then to Lory's office. Finding no sign of her, he went to check her flat. When he reached the flat, it was clear that somebody was inside; the door was wide open. He entered, calling to Lory, and when he got to the bedroom he could hear Lory crying. He knocked gently on the door, entered, and found Lory lying on her stomach on the bed. Sitting down beside her, Nick gently caressed her head and asked, "What's the matter?"

"Everything," Lory responded in an absolutely miserable voice.

"I don't understand. What happened? Why are you crying so helplessly?"

"I've been suffering for months. I've just hidden my sorrow. I can't go on like this any longer," Lory admitted in final desperation.

"For months? I never realized."

"Yup. I'm a natural born actress. I guess I missed my calling," Lory responded sarcastically.

"I have no idea what's causing you so much sorrow, but you definitely deserve an Oscar for your daily performance."

"Thanks," Lory responded, whimpering, as she accepted the handkerchief Nick offer her to dry her eyes.

"But seriously, what's going on? Has something happened to your parents? Is there anything I can do? For God's sake, say something," Nick began to push her.

"No, it's not my parents. I really don't know if I should tell you. Especially now, with your news about your engagement."

"What's my engagement got to do with any of this, Lory? I'm totally confused."

"Well, OK. Here's the story. Greg doesn't love me. He refuses all physical contact with me while saying he loves me and that everything is all right. But I believe he's really gay."

"What? That's really difficult. What do you plan to do?"

"I plan to divorce him. I just wish I knew how to persuade him to accept it. Luckily, we only had a civil service, so I don't feel bound to him for the rest of my life in the eyes of God."

At that moment, the phone rang. It was Gigi calling to tell her that Veltmann needed her to come back to the conference immediately. Her conversation with Nick interrupted, Lory fixed her make up and they went together, back to the conference hall. The coffee break was still in progress, so they arrived just in time. To ensure that she met Veltmann's expectations, Lory worked tirelessly all day and retired only after the last guests had returned to their hotels. That evening, conference attendees had dinner on their own, since the Institute was hosting a reception the next day to end the conference. So, Lory spent the evening with unsuspecting Greg, who still showed no recognition of the meltdown of their marriage. In fact, he announced that Leslie would be coming to spend a a week with them. Lory, reeling from the announcement, could not hold back her irritation.

"Don't you think you should have asked me before you invited him?"

"My dear, I knew you wouldn't refuse and would welcome him with joy."

"I probably wouldn't have refused him, but I wouldn't have invited him either," Lory responded, angrily.

"Well, that settles it, right? He's arriving on Saturday."

"Nice," Lory said, heading to the kitchen to distract herself by making dinner.

They ate their dinner in silence, after which they prepared to retired and read a bit before going to bed.

The following day was the last day of the conference. As usual, the Institute provided a buffet lunch at noon, so participants could enjoy the afternoon session refreshed and well fed. The Institute also organized a grand reception to close out the conference. Throughout the day, Lory was responsible for encouraging communication among the guests, sometimes introducing them to one another. In spite of how busy she was, Nick found a moment when she was free and got directly to the point.

"Lory, you still haven't explained how I'm concerned in your issues with Greg. Please don't be opaque. I need to understand."

"All right. I will tell you everything, but not now. By the time the reception is over, we will be too exhausted. Can I come to you flat tomorrow at lunch so we can talk? Will that work?"

"Yes. Tomorrow at lunch will have to be soon enough, but not a minute later."

"Good. Don't worry," Lory responded, just as Veltmann was approaching her with one of the speakers.

Later, during the reception, Lory saw Greg talking cheerfully with Phil and the Caretaker's daughter, Isabella. Eventually, she noticed he'd gotten tired and signaled his intention to retire. Lory responded by nodding her head with an artificial smile. By the time she arrived home, Greg was sleeping deeply. Under a hot shower, she realized that her life had arrived at a turning point. If she told Nick everything tomorrow, there would be nothing left to save her marriage. Then she asked herself if she really wanted to save her bad marriage. Her immediate answer surprised her. Yes, she still wanted to save her marriage. She still desired to be loved by her husband and to make love to him as a married couple. But just as quickly, she realized it was impossible and that she was waiting and hoping in vain. Afterall, her husband was more interested in courting Leslie Talbot than his own wife. It was clear to her that Greg used her as cover and because he wanted to have children someday.

Greg spent the following day at the university. Meanwhile, the conference ended and the speakers were transported to the airport, so, it was easy for Lory to meet Nick for lunch, undisturbed.

"Come in! May I offer you anything? Are you hungry?" Nick invited her to eat something with him once she arrived.

"Thank you, but I don't have an appetite. Maybe after we talk."

"All right. But I made tea for you. The water is boiling, so will you take a nice hot cup of tea?" he asked while bringing two cups to the living room and pouring tea into them.

"Thanks. I guess I should start," Lory said, preparing for her confession, steaming cup of tea in hand.

"Please, do," Nick encouraged her sitting in an armchair beside her.

"Well, please don't think I'm an imposter or capricious. My actions and decisions were motivated by other reason."

"Of course not, Lory! I wouldn't think that of you in my wildest dreams. How can you even think that?"

"You say that now, but you don't know the whole story."

"Believe me, no matter what you tell me, I won't think those things of you. So please, tell me your story. I'd really like hear it."

"Then, please listen." Lory started her story with her unexpected, sincere and immense love for Nick, followed by the attractive and openhearted but a somewhat blackmailing proposal Greg made on New Year's Eve. Then she described in detail the last year's surprising events and the deepening conflict within her marriage, including all the ups and downs of her emotional state, the many disappointments and the heart ache. After she finished they sat side by side for what seemed like an eternity to Lory.

"I know everything is my fault. I shouldn't have married Greg. Now I will divorce him and start over again. Alone," Lory said, revealing everything what she felt deep in her heart before Nick could speak. But he didn't wait long to respond.

"Oh, no Lory! Don't blame yourself! You're the victim in this saga. I am so sorry. If I had known or suspected the truth…but who would imagine something like this? Don't worry, we will solve this together. You are not alone. You must believe me!"

"But what about Caroline? I don't want to destroy your happiness, too!"

"Come on, don't be ridiculous. You are my happiness! I know it sounds cruel, but she was only a substitute. It's for the best that she also have the chance to find real love, which she could never find with me. My heart has been yours from the start."

Lory began to cry with relief and happiness, still unable to not fully accept in her heart. She pulled herself together and said, "I love you so much! Please lead the way, because I don't have the strength to fight for or lead anything right now. It will take all my strength to divorce Greg and inform my parents of my situation."

"All right, my dear! Trust me." and Nick pulled Lory to him and kissed her passionately.

CHAPTER TWENTY-TWO

The Moment of the Truth

That evening Lory could barely wait for Greg to come home. When he arrived home she invited him for a drink.

"How kind of you, my love. You haven't done this in a long time."

"We have a serious topic to discuss. I know about your relationship with Leslie Talbot and I am not inclined to act as a cover for your homosexual tendencies any longer."

"What are you talking about?"

"Everybody has their right to real love. You've let me down. You don't love me. At least not in the way a man loves his wife. I had to accept that you would never be a passionate lover, and I've given up trying to make a conquest of you."

"You are delirious? Are you a fool? I truly am in love with you!"

"Then why do you cast me off? You won't even kiss me in casual greeting. Other women are kissed by their husbands all the time. You only make love to me twice a year. That is simply ridiculous!"

"What about my parents? They love you as you like a daughter. They invited you to Japan and we could travel the rest of the world together."

"Yes. Like brothers and sister, or two friends. I am sorry, but I want more. I want my emotions reciprocated."

"So, marrying me didn't mean anything to you?"

"If you had told me the truth about you, I would never have married you. You made me discover the truth by myself, and now divorce is the only way out of this situation."

"How dare you accuse me of homosexuality? Are you going mad? You've already made up your mind, haven't you? Fine, I won't get in your way. If you don't love me anymore, it's better we separate. Now, I will never have children. I am disappointed in our marriage."

"I agree. I'd like you to find another flat as soon as possible, so we can begin our official separation."

"But I just ask Leslie to come here to visit us here. I promised to invite him and his lover, Steve, in return for the Canary Islands."

"Oh my God! What are we, a hotel? You never mentioned when we went to Tenerife that it was some kind of exchange program! I don't want them in my home, especially not right now! When do they arrive?"

"Next Saturday."

"That's impossible! Call off the invitation!"

"But what will I tell them? To them, we are a dream couple."

"Oh, clearly a 'dream couple' means something totally different to you and me. I'm not even sure you know its real meaning! As far as I'm concerned, you can tell them anything you want, but I suggest you tell them the truth."

"Don't you understand? You are more than a woman to me. I love your soul!"

"I want to be loved, totally, emotionally and physically, not just my soul, which seems to be the only thing you love."

"Most men would only love you physically! Isn't it better to have a transcendent love?"

"It might have have been enough for me, if you hadn't gotten into a compromising situation with Leslie in Tenerife. From that moment, I couldn't trust you. And I cannot live with an unreliable man."

"What compromising situation are you talking about?"

"Please, don't pretend to be innocent! The last week we were there, you went upstairs during the siesta to talk to Leslie. I went up to join you half an hour later and found the apartment empty except for the bedroom."

"Oh, I am so sorry!"

"So, you admit it."

"Well, yes, there was something between us, but only attraction, not like with you. You are my soulmate!"

"So, a soulmate doesn't deserve physical faithfulness? I deserve a spouse to be both my spiritual and physical soulmate. Maybe I want too much, but I won't give up looking for it! Just leave me alone and move on!"

At that moment the telephone rang. It was Lory's parents, ending the conversation with Greg, who moved into the spare room for the night.

The next morning at breakfast the atmosphere was frosty. Lory could hardly wait for Greg to leave for work so she could go to her office. As soon as she arrived and sat in her chair, Nick came in and kissed her. They could barely leave one another to start work. Holding Lory around the waist, Nick whispered to her, "We have to spend some time together every day, otherwise I'll go crazy!"

"Yes! I feel the same way. I can't go through the divorce without you!"

"Don't worry we will get through it together. But I need to go to Amsterdam for the weekend to talk to Caroline. I've got to do it in person. You understand, don't you?"

"Of course. I will survive, somehow."

"I will be back on Monday. Also, Veltmann approves."

"Great. We are moving forward!"

"And we will never stop. But now, I have to go to work. Let's not share our relationship with everyone yet."

"I agree. We will tell them, after we've taken care of a few things." Nick turned to Lory for a good-bye kiss, then left in hurry.

The day passed quickly and Lory prepared herself for another evening conversation with her husband. Greg was a bit late, and greeted Lory with a pale face.

"How were things at work?" Lory asked.

"Are you serious? I can hardly concentrate because of our what you said last night."

"I'm sorry, but I have hardly been able to concentrate on my work for months, because of the way you cast off me. You made me feel undesirable, with no consequences for you. But you must have known things weren't going well for me!"

"I understand, now, and I am so sorry. I really am very sorry! I will never have a family and children."

"You can never know."

"But I know it."

"All the same, it would be better if you admitted that you're in love with Leslie and don't torment other women! By the way, I hope you talked to Leslie, so he won't come here with his actual lover!"

"I spoke to Veltmann and he's willing to give them the guest flat at the Institute."

"That's nice," she responded sarcastically. "So, they're coming anyway."

"You won't have to deal with them. I'll take care of them."

"I hope so. But, knowing you, you'll want to invite them for dinner with us at least once or twice, won't you?"

"Well, yes, at least for one dinner. It will be the best way to inform them about our divorce."

"OK, but only one dinner. And I will not be showing them the city."

"All right. You don't have to. I'll take care of everything. I'll take a few days off that week."

For the rest of the week, they barely exchanged a word until the arrival of Greg's gay friends. Leslie was a charming and polite middle-aged man and his lover, Steve, was a slim and delicate dancer. They occupied the guest flat with pleasure, and came to Lory's flat for dinner the first evening. The news of Lory and Greg's divorce stunned them.

"I never imagined the two of you would divorce!" Leslie said, while eating the fettucine. "You are the perfect couple. You simply can't give up!"

"It's decided. There is no going back," Greg responding, knowing his wife's state of mind.

After dinner Leslie went to the balcony to smoke a cigarette. Lory joined him, bringing an ashtray.

"Lory, what's the real reason for the divorce? You can tell me. It's the lack of physical intimacy, isn't it?

"Well, yes that's one of the problems. He has cast me off millions of times and he doesn't desire me at all."

"But you knew that he was gay, didn't you? You don't have to divorce him because of it. You can always keep a lover."

"No, I didn't know. And I won't keep a lover. I won't get mixed up in adultery. If our marriage can't go on in a sincere and honest way, then each of us needs to follow our own path." She turned on her heel and returned to the flat, clearing the table. The only reason she didn't cry was because she kept thinking about Nick, who at that moment was informing Caroline about their situation. The thought that Nick would soon be free warmed her heart and made it easier for her not to be bothered by what was happening around her.

Lory lived the following days with complete apathy, concentrating only on the fact that she had to share the news with her parents and her brother, Steve. Luckily, they understood her choice, immediately. In reality there was little else they could do, once she gave them all the facts.

"I didn't want to tell you over the phone, mom, but Veltmann wouldn't give me any days off, right now. He gave Nick a few days to go to Amsterdam to clear the way for our future together, which is more important right now. But, as a result, I can't leave the Institute."

"I see, my little one. Don't worry! You know, it's interesting. Your dad doesn't always have the best instincts when it comes to people, but this time he was right. He noticed the first time he shook hands with Greg that something was off. He said Greg's handshake was too soft and not masculine enough."

"Really? He never mentioned that to me!"

"Well, you know your father. He would never speak ill of anyone you loved, and at the time, you really loved Greg."

"That's true. My dear daddy!"

"And there were all those gifts Greg gave you. Your dad said, 'All these gifts are to compensate for something.'"

"That's amazing! I would never have thought that daddy would have had such great insight into Greg's character!"

"Now, my dear, focus on yourself. We all are on your side. You'll see everything's going to be all right!" Then they said good-bye to one another.

The one person Lory didn't worry about telling, was her brother. She was sure that knowing the details of her life, Steve would defend her completely.

"You know, little sister, I'll beat him up if you want."

"No, Steve. Thank you, but that's not necessary."

"Do you want me to come get you? Can you manage all this tension?"

"Yes, I can. Thanks, but you don't have to bring me home, either. I am so grateful, though, for your willingness. I love you!"

"I love you, too, sister! Just say the word and I'll be there to get you!"

All these words had a positive effect on Lory's mood. She felt much stronger and focused only on her future life with Nick.

As Nick had predicted, breaking it off with Caroline and cancelling their engagement was not easy. Nick used all his persuasion, but, unfortunately, Caroline refused to let go. But her resistance had the opposite result of what she intended. Nick didn't even want to stay friends with her. Finally, he broke off their engagement and returned to Rome, feeling lighter, to inform Lory that he was free. Lory wrapped her arms around his neck joyfully. Then she told him about her family's reactions to her decision. Greg had moved to another flat, so Lory and Nick were able spend the night together. They began to plan their wedding and their future life. The decided to get married in Rome, celebrating with their families, relatives, friends and colleagues.

CHAPTER TWENTY-THREE

The Wedding

The Big Day arrived sooner than they anticipated. Rome in June was the most perfect scene for their wedding, which they held in the Church of Santa Maria in Ara Coeli. After the ceremony the newlyweds and their guests went to Anzio where they had an excellent party in the ornate garden of a well-appointed restaurant. They were filled with joy and their infectious happiness spread to all of their guests.

Lory and Nick decided to spend their honeymoon in Corfu. So, the next morning they started a joyful trip toward the marvelous island and toward their future together.

The author

Szilvia Gresina was born in Balassagyarmat, Hungary on the 12th of October in 1970. She obtained her MA graduation in Sociology at the „Eötvös Lórand" University of Sciences in Budapest, then got another Master degree at the University of Sciences „La Sapienza" in Rome. Afterwards she has worked for the Hungarian Academy in Rome for five years and then as a researcher for the European University Institute for European Studies in Triest for seven years. Her hobbies are yoga, fitness, reading, films, gardening, music, arts, trekking. She speaks English, Italian and German launguages. Her Godparents are Italian. She is officially engaged. Her skills in writing are based on her experiences got in journalism writing life-interviews and articles for the local paper „KéK Forrás" (Blue Spring) and an e-book entitled „The World of Etruscans" pubblished in 2013.